NANCY PEARL
PRESENTS
A BOOK CRUSH REDISCOVERY

Best Friends

by Mary Bard

two lions

two lions

Published by Two Lions, New York

www.apub.com

Amazon, the Amazon logo, and Two Lions
are trademarks of Amazon.com, Inc., or its affiliates.

"Fireflies," which appears on page 185, is copyright © 1924 by Perry Mason Company.

ISBN-13: 9781477827161 (hardcover)
ISBN-10: 1477827161 (hardcover)
ISBN-13: 9781477821138 (paperback)
ISBN-10: 1477821139 (paperback)

Book design by Virginia Pope

Library of Congress Control Number: 2014914205

Printed in the United States of America

Contents

Introduction by Nancy Pearl

Of all the hundreds of books that I read when I was in the fifth and sixth grades—and reading is pretty much all that I ever did back then (not so different from now, truth be told)—the book that has stayed with me in the most vivid detail is Mary Bard's *Best Friends*. I suspect that the reason for this is that at the time I couldn't think of anything I wanted more than to live in the world inhabited by the characters of Bard's story.

On the surface, the circumstances of Suzie Green's life seemed entirely different from my own. I lived in a two-family home in a lower-middle-class neighborhood on Detroit's near northwest side (my family lived upstairs while my aunt and uncle and their two sons lived downstairs), while Suzie's house was in a leafy section of Seattle among other large one-family homes. I lived with my father, mother, and younger sister; as I remember it, none of us were particularly happy. Suzie lived with her young and attractive widowed mother, who teaches at Suzie's school, along with her healthy and young-at-heart grandparents, who adore their granddaughter and are very involved in her life. Grandmother baked wonderful pies and tasty cookies and made delicious fried chicken for special dinners. Best of all, when Suzie turned seven, Grandfather built an amazing tree house for her; on every succeeding birthday he added new wonders to Suzie's lookout.

How I envied Suzie that tree house! There was nothing at that time that I desired more. There was an apricot tree in my backyard, a space that was bordered on one side by an alley, where we weren't allowed to play, and on another, by a lot where five or six huge trucks were seemingly permanently parked. I regularly climbed that apricot tree and would curl up in the branches and read until I could no longer ignore how painfully uncomfortable sitting there was.

But for all the differences in our outer circumstances, inwardly we seemed not so dissimilar. I shared Suzie's frustration at school, her growing interest in boys, and her conflicted feelings over being a tomboy. And, most of all, we both wanted, with all our hearts, a true best friend.

What kept me reading and rereading *Best Friends* was my unspoken wish to leave my unexciting, bleak, and unsatisfactory (or so it seemed to my ten-year-old self) behind, and reappear in Suzie's world—to be Suzie and live her life.

Even if I knew that it wasn't really possible to do that, to become Suzie, at least for the time that I was reading the book I could achieve what I wanted. My childhood response to Bard's novel describes what I've long believed about books for young people: a child needs to be able simultaneously to see him or herself *and* lose her or himself in the pages of a book.

Perhaps it makes sense to think of books for children and teens on a continuum that stretches from books that allow readers to find themselves, to those that make it easy for readers to lose themselves in. In recent years, non-genre literature for children and teens has moved steadily toward hyper-realism, depicting children and teens in all sorts of difficult situations. That's not a bad thing at all; there are real children in the real world living in all kinds of terrible, painful-to-contemplate situations. There are children who live with abusive parents, or who are forced to move from one inadequate foster home to another. There are children whose father or mother is away serving in a war somewhere across the world, and then comes home a changed person. Or dies in some foreign country. There are, of course, many children who are living in poverty, or who are immigrants, legal or illegal, their families looking for a better life across the border. There are children who are confused about their sexuality. There are children with a parent who's incarcerated.

All young readers deserve to find, need to find, books that reflect their particular situations. That's the "find themselves" part of the continuum. At the other edge of the continuum are those books that many young readers can most easily and deeply lose themselves in. When we think of those sorts of books, of the phenomena of "losing oneself" in a book, we're usually referring to fantasy novels and the invented worlds of elves, wizards, swords, dragons, and sorcery: the whole good vs. evil dynamic. There are many, many young readers who will tell you that they felt they, too, were rescued by the Ents when they, along with Merry and Pippin, were lost in Mirkwood, or that they'd spent time in Narnia, or could describe down to the minutest detail the world of Hogwarts and what it was like to live there.

But the books that do both, books in which readers can identify with the characters and at the same time find themselves drawn into a life significantly different from their own, tend to be the most memorable reading experiences. I believe children need to read books that offer different ways people can behave, describe different choices people can make, and demonstrate what ordinary happiness might look like. Family stories like *Best Friends* or Carol Ryrie Brink's *Family Grandstand* and *Family Sabbatical* give young readers an escape from as well as a pathway to "real" life. When, at age ten, I read *Best Friends*, I think that I, unconsciously, laid out a plan for myself about the kind of life I wanted to live and the type of parent I wanted to be. On the surface, Mary Bard's *Best Friends* might not seem to be particularly profound, but reading it certainly gave me a direction in my life that I hadn't had before. One simple example is a game that Suzie and her friends play at her birthday party. It's a game I never played as a child, and I've never seen it described in any other book. But when I discovered it in the pages of *Best Friends*, I never forgot it. My children have happy memories of playing it at their birthday parties (we called it "Spiderweb"). And just a few years ago, we played it at one of my granddaughter's parties as well.

Such is the power of reading.

Chapter One

The Pink House

One blowy March afternoon Suzie Green slammed out the back door, stamped down the steps, and ran through the orchard muttering, "How would Grandmother like it if there wasn't anybody her age in the whole darned neighborhood. I don't care what she says—I just hate Millicent! I'm never going to speak to her again as long as I live!"

Suzie's cheeks were bright pink, her eyes were swimming with tears, and her words were like short, angry explosions. "Honestly! With all the schools in Seattle, Millicent would have to choose ours to ruin! It's bad enough to be the only person in our room who hasn't any best friend. Oh, what's the use? I could just scream!"

She vaulted the hedge at the foot of the orchard and ran blindly toward the big madroña tree which held her

Lookout. Meanwhile Jet, Grandfather's black Labrador hunting dog, galloped along beside her whining and trying to thrust his nose into her hand. She jerked away from him. "Oh, stop it, Jet. Nobody understands! Not one single soul!" She grabbed the ladder and began to climb, stamping her feet on each rung. "There's one sure thing—Millicent and her old Select Seven will never—ever—put—one—toe—on—my—Lookout!" Jet, groaning and protesting, followed her up the ladder.

When she reached the platform, she sat down cross-legged and curled herself against Jet's warm velvety side. She brushed the tears away with the back of her hand, reached in the pocket of her jeans, took out an apple and crunched a big juicy bite. "Count my blessings! Stop feeling sorry for myself! I'd just like to know how Grandmother would feel if she had to sit behind Millicent and hear her whisper, 'Suzie's teacher's pe-et. Suzie's teacher's pe-et.' Honestly! It makes me so darned mad!"

Suzie chewed her apple and continued to mutter about how much she hated everything and everybody. In spite of herself she began to watch the great fir trees in the garden below her lean toward one another and sigh in the warm spring wind. "Even the trees—always whispering," she grumbled. Wisps of cloud raced across the bright blue sky and long gray wind rifts streaked the surface of the lake. It was Suzie's favorite kind of day—blustery one moment and shining and still the next. She watched the patterns in the clouds for a while, and finally heaved a long shuddery sigh. "Oh well, I'm still thankful for the Lookout."

Suzie's Lookout was certainly something to be thankful for. It was her own secret hideaway where she spent every afternoon after school and where she kept her favorite things. Grandfather had built the original platform for her as a surprise for her seventh birthday. On each birthday after that, he had added more equipment, until now it was almost as neat and convenient as the wheelhouse of a ship. There were the canvas hood, which she could pull over the top when it rained, and the navy hammock. When she was lazily swinging back and forth she could look clear across Lake Washington to the snow-tipped Cascade Mountains and pretend she was a sea gull or an airplane stewardess.

There were waterproofed fish boxes around the edge of the platform which made cupboards and bookcases where she kept her letters, stories, poems, paints, and drawing tablets, her agate collection and her shell collection as well as her joke books, comics, and movie magazines. The cupboards could all be locked with one key. Her mother had given her a silver chain so she could wear the key around her neck and never lose it.

But the thing Suzie liked best of all about her Lookout was that she could look down on the Pink

House and see every corner of its large hedged garden. In fact, the Pink House was the blessing that Suzie always counted next, after the Lookout. Ever since she could remember, it had stood under the tall whispery trees, with shutters closed and doors locked, like an exciting Christmas present, ready and almost begging to be opened.

Before she had the Lookout she had spent every afternoon trying to catch the goldfish in the pool. She would run up and down the paths, and peek through the closed shutters, trying to find out what the inside of the Pink House looked like. Lately she had spent all her time pretending that movie stars lived in there and she was their very best friend. There were a father and a mother and a little girl, who was exactly Suzie's age, now eleven going on twelve. Sometimes she pretended they were so busy making movies that they couldn't come back to the Pink House, but they always invited her down to Hollywood to visit them. Sometimes she pretended that they gave enormous parties, and she spent hours and hours drawing beautiful formals with slippers to match for all the movie stars to wear.

Gusts of wind played with Suzie's hair and blew cool little breaths against her flushed cheeks. "I'm even getting sick and tired of pretending about the people in the Pink House. I wish somebody real would . . ."

Jet moved restlessly and growled.

"What's the matter with you?" Suzie absent-mindedly rubbed Jet's ear. He growled again, and she stood up and looked down at the Pink House. A man was folding back the outside shutters, and from inside the house, someone was pulling up the blinds and opening the windows. "Heavens to Betsy! They must be spring cleaning. No—oh my gosh!" Suzie couldn't believe her eyes. A big yellow moving van was backing slowly down the driveway toward a convertible and two smaller trucks. Suzie hastily climbed out onto the long limb of the madroña tree. "Somebody must be moving in!"

Suzie's heart pounded with excitement as she watched a tall dark man come around the house and stand in the patio below her, directing two workmen. "I think we'd better start with the pool and then repair the tennis court. It'll probably need resurfacing. We'll be using the pool for swimming this year, and I want to be sure there are no rough places on the bottom."

Suzie held Jet's collar so he wouldn't bark and whispered, "Gosh! He's going to turn it into a regular Hollywood swimming pool!"

The pool had always been Suzie's favorite place to play. It was large and irregular, almost like a tiny lake. It was shaped like a figure eight and had natural rock edges, and was lined with blue tiles. At the small end where it was deep, there was a little stone Japanese bridge overhung by a big weeping willow. She had waded in the shallow end, but she hadn't explored the deep end under the bridge because there were tubs of wavy green water plants that floated out and curled around her legs and made her shudder.

Jet began to growl again. Suzie said, "Hush! I want to hear what they're saying." She wound her legs around the branch and listened breathlessly to all sorts of exciting plans for pruning the trees, cutting back the shrubs, planting the flower beds, and making the garden happy and bright.

Suzie hugged herself and wriggled ecstatically. Suddenly "The Afternoon of a Faun" poured from a record player inside the house. The music seemed to run along her arms and all down her back the way it did at the Children's Symphony.

The tall dark man walked quickly across the patio and opened the front door. "Clothilde? Co Co? May I speak to you, please?" The music stopped, and a girl just about Suzie's size came out the front door. "Oui, Papa. You wish to speak with me?"

Suzie kicked her feet and a book fell off the cupboard, bounced through the thick branches, and landed on the ground.

The little girl turned and looked toward the place where Suzie was lying. "What is that? Papa, do the Americans then live in the trees?"

The man smiled down at her. "Of course not, Co Co. What makes you think they do?"

Co Co pointed toward the Lookout. "There, Papa— I don't see double. The book there—it fell from the tree."

Her father laughed and put his arm around her. "Co Co, you are imagining again."

Co Co frowned. "No, Papa. There is something in the tree. Tomorrow, after lunch, I will climb up and see what is there."

Then Suzie almost said, "Heavens to Betsy," right out loud, for they began to speak in a foreign language. They spoke so rapidly that it sounded sputtery, like little Chinese firecrackers.

Suzie watched every move they made as they walked back and forth in the patio below her, and listened as hard as she could, but she couldn't understand what they were saying. Suddenly Co Co stopped right below her. She put her hands on her hips and faced her father. "Oui, Papa, you say 'un moment, un moment' but you do not go. Mademoiselle tells me she wishes to go back to the hotel immediately. She is in a bad humor. Could you come quick please, or she will scold me."

Co Co's father laughed and leaned over and kissed her on the tip of her nose. "Oui, chèrie. Yes, I'll come quickly. I, too, fear Mademoiselle's scolding."

Co Co chuckled, a delightful, friendly sound, and

Suzie almost laughed with her. She looked and sounded like the most interesting little girl Suzie had ever seen. Her black hair hung straight to her shoulders, and her bangs were cut to a point in the middle of her forehead. She wore her dark-blue beret perched flat on the top of her head, her coat was straight with a little white collar, and she wore white gloves, white socks, and black patent leather slippers with low heels. When she spoke English her words were slow and careful, like a grown person reading aloud.

Co Co's father spoke in English as he told all the things he was planning to do in the garden. Co Co nodded her head and said, "Oui, oui—yes, that will be good," and reminded him again and again that Mademoiselle would scold if they did not hurry. Finally they linked arms and went in the house, and the door of the Pink House closed behind them.

"Boy, this is really neat!" As Suzie listened to the hum of vacuum cleaners, the swish of windows being thrown open, and the shouts of the moving men as they carried in huge crates, she was trying to think what their strange language reminded her of. Suddenly she remembered the French songs on the radio. "That's it. Her father called her 'chèrie'—they must be French. Oh boy! This is lots better than anything I ever pretended."

Jet growled again, and Suzie watched Co Co and

her father and a tall thin lady, dressed all in black, come out the front door and walk around the back of the house. The tall thin lady was also speaking French, but she was shaking her head and sounded as if she might be giving Co Co and her father the promised scolding. Suzie giggled sympathetically as she watched Co Co nodding obediently and saying, "Oui, Mademoiselle," over and over again. Then they all got in the convertible and drove off down the driveway.

Jet began to whine and Suzie looked at her wrist watch. "It's after five and Grandmother will be cross. Mother will be home, and I haven't set the table or made the salad." She backed rapidly down the ladder and raced back across the orchard with Jet.

She banged open the kitchen door and gasped, "Guess what!"

Grandmother was standing with her back to Suzie, stirring something on the stove. "I don't have to guess. You have no more sense of time than a cricket."

Suzie said, "I'm sorry I'm late, but just wait 'til I tell you why. Mother, I'll bet you can't ever guess what's happened!"

Suzie's mother was sitting at the kitchen table correcting papers and drinking a cup of tea. She smiled at Suzie and said, "Come over and give me a big kiss. My, you have pink cheeks! What have you been doing?"

Suzie rushed over and hugged her mother. "You'll just never believe it, but a man who looks exactly like a movie star is really moving into the Pink House, only his wife doesn't look like a movie star—she looks like a thin black crane and has eyebrows clear across her forehead and they have a little girl and her name is Clothilde only they call her 'Co Co' and she has straight black hair and bangs and she says 'eet' instead of 'it' and 'weeth' instead of 'with' only she speaks half English and half French and she sounds just like those French songs on the radio and . . ."

Grandmother said, "Slow down, Suzie, slow down. You're talking like an express train. I hate to interrupt you, but Mother has to go to a meeting and the table must be set."

Suzie rushed into the pantry and began to grab knives and forks, talking steadily, "And they're making the pool into a regular Hollywood swimming pool and planting all sorts of flowers and it's going to be just gorgeous. Oh, this is the most exciting day of my whole life!"

She stopped in front of her mother. "One thing I am disappointed about. I hoped her mother would have blond curly hair and dark-blue eyes and dimples and be pretty the way you are, but Mademoiselle, which is what Co Co calls her, looks as if she didn't even know how to smile. Why, she even wears a kind of a black wedding veil."

Suzie's mother laughed. "If Co Co calls her 'Mademoiselle,' she probably isn't her mother."

"Well, I hope not because both Co Co and her father look just darling and Mademoiselle has pinchy lips and a pointed nose and sounds kind of like a cross teacher. . . ." Suzie clapped her hand over her mouth. "I'm sorry—but you never sound like a cross teacher. You're always just darling. No wonder everybody in school says you are the prettiest teacher in the whole city. I wish Co Co's mother looked exactly like you."

Grandmother said, "And you're as alike as two peas in a pod, Suzie. Now for heaven's sake, let's get the table set and the salad made, or your mother will never get to that meeting."

Suzie started to make the salad, and her mother finished setting the table. While they worked Suzie told about the tennis court and the patio and repeated every word that Co Co and her father had said, except the French words.

When Grandfather came in he said, "I hear Bill Langdon's back in town. I'd better go over there tomorrow and see what I can do to help him."

That started Suzie off again, and she told her Grandfather a thoroughly mixed-up account of the afternoon, ending with, "Please, Grandfather, may I go with you when you go over there? I want to talk to Co Co. Please—please?"

Grandfather said, "We'll see, Suziekins, we'll see," and began to read the paper.

Suzie's mother said quietly, "I think it would be best, Suzie, to wait until after Grandfather talks to Mr. Langdon."

"Ohhhh, Mo-o-ther!" Suzie wailed.

Grandmother said, "I'll certainly be interested to hear what Bill Langdon has to say about letting that house stand vacant all these years. Not one word. Perfectly ridiculous waste of money, not to speak of the housing shortage." She glanced at Suzie, who was now listening so hard her mouth was open. "I won't go into it because little pitchers have big ears."

Suzie said, "Ohhhh, Grandmother!" and wished for the hundredth time that Grandmother would not call her a pitcher the minute the conversation became really interesting.

She leaned over and whispered to her mother, "Is Co Co's father, Bill Langdon?"

Her mother nodded. "I think so, darling. Now, eat your dinner."

That was another thing—Suzie wished grown people would not say, "Eat your dinner." They talked and talked and sometimes ate so slowly that they were at the table long after she was in bed, but they always said, "Eat your dinner," to her, the moment the conversation was so interesting she could hardly swallow. She heaved a large sigh and said, "Honestly!" and slowly chewed one cold string bean.

She put down her fork. "Grandmother, I hope I'm not being rude, but when you were almost twelve, did you like to be called 'a little pitcher'?"

Grandmother tried to look stern, but her face was twitching with suppressed laughter as she answered, "No, Suzie, indeed I did not, and I liked even less to hear 'Children should be seen and not heard,' although goodness knows I heard it often enough."

"Are you mad at Mr. Langdon?"

"No, but it's just one of those things I'd prefer not to discuss. When it comes right down to it, I guess my feelings are hurt. Bill Langdon's just like my own son, and not one word all these years. I'll certainly give him a chance to explain but . . ."

Suzie's mother broke in, "Suzie, Bill Langdon is just your uncle Jim's age. We used to play together all the time when we were children. I think Grandmother thought we might get married when we grew up. Actually Bill always treated me like a little sister—not a date."

"A date! Heavens to Betsy!" Suzie looked at her mother and tried to imagine her having a date.

Her mother grinned and continued. "Bill went East to college, and then after he graduated he went to Europe with an oil company. He married a French girl, and I imagine Co Co is probably their child."

Suzie stared thoughtfully at her mother. "And you went to the University and learned to be a teacher and married Daddy and had me. But I still don't see why I can't play with Co Co."

Grandfather cleared his throat. "We'll let bygones be bygones and be as neighborly as we always have been."

Suzie's mother said, "Perhaps it would be just as well not to mention the Langdons at school, until after we have talked to them, Suzie."

Suzie promised and crossed her heart. But she could almost see Millicent and the Select Seven gasping with envy when she stood in the center of the group during recess and told them all about Co Co and her father and the Hollywood swimming pool. She thought, *That's the trouble with secrets. The minute you hear one, you always think of all the people you could tell it to.* She made an extra cross on her heart and bit the tip of her finger to remind her not to tell one soul.

Suzie's mother smiled. "Come on, darling. I must get to that meeting."

Suzie picked up two plates and stared at her mother. "Did you and Mr. Langdon go steady, Mother?"

Her mother didn't answer for a minute, and there was a dimply smile on her face as she said, "No, Suzie. We used to swim and sail and dance together. I had a crush on him, but he probably never thought of me except as Jim's little sister. He used to call me 'Pest,' to be perfectly honest with you."

Suzie slowly wandered back and forth, trying to imagine what it would be like if her mother had married Mr. Langdon. "Would we have lived in the Pink House, Mother?" she asked.

"I doubt it. Bill's family tore down the old house and built that one after Bill went to Europe. When they died, he came back and closed the house and said he never wanted to see it again. Now, stop moving like a snail. By the way, how did your May poster turn out?"

The mention of the May poster reminded Suzie of Millicent and the Select Seven and being called teacher's pet and all of her hurts and slights. Immediately her mouth turned down and she said dramatically, "Don't be surprised if our whole room gets expelled. Today was just terrible. Millicent—well, I'll bet you just can't imagine what happened!"

Suzie's mother took Suzie's chin in her hand and said, "Let me see, I imagine that the firebell rang and Millicent stood in front of the door and wouldn't let anyone out and the smoke began to curl and the flames to crackle."

Suzie smiled but she continued in the same whiney, dramatic voice, "You just don't know. Millicent was just awful." Her voice rose as she stalked into the dining room. "And that wasn't the worst. Right in the middle of science, Miss Morrison announced that she isn't coming back next year." She swished over and flapped a dish towel. "I could give you a million guesses and you'd never guess why. Miss Morrison—is—going—to—get—married!"

"So she told me. Isn't that wonderful?"

"Mother! Honestly! I'll have you know Miss Morrison is going to marry a principal. If that isn't just about the craziest thing anybody ever heard of. Honestly!"

"Why, Suzie, what's wrong with that? Everybody likes Mr. Wagner."

"Mother! In the first place he's a principal, and in the second place, he's so old!"

Suzie's mother laughed. "He isn't very old, Suzie. He's just about my age, and I'm still able to creep around a little. We all think it's a wonderful idea. They have so much in common, and they've known each other for ages."

"It's all very well for you to laugh, Mother, but nobody your age gets married."

"Oh, come now! What about all those movie stars?"

"That's different. They're glamorous, but not teachers and principals. That's ab-so-lute-ly im-pos-sible! And another thing . . ." As Suzie dried each dish she added another highly exaggerated account of all the awful things that happened in school.

Finally Suzie's mother said, "You're not behaving one bit like yourself lately, Suziekins. What is really bothering you?"

Suzie was quiet for a long time while she tried to think of some way to tell her mother why she felt so crabby and whiney. You certainly couldn't tell your own mother that you wished more than anything she wasn't a teacher. The Select Seven said it certainly was neat to have your mother do all your homework and see that you got good grades and never got caught at anything. But it wasn't neat—it was just awful. If she tried to act polite and quiet and get good grades so her mother wouldn't be embarrassed, they called her "teacher's pet." If she tried to act smarty and not study, they whispered, "Suzie Green thinks she's smart. *She* can get away with murder. *Her* mother's a teacher. Pretty neat!"

Anyway she didn't feel one bit like herself. She felt like three different people. The Suzie who went to school was so mixed-up and scared she didn't dare raise her hand. The Select Seven were so mean she just stood around on the playground by herself wishing she were bossy and boy crazy like Millicent.

Practically the only time she didn't want to be like Millicent was when they were having sports. Rich and Ray both said she pitched like a boy. When she was riding her bike or climbing trees she certainly didn't want to be an old scaredy cat like Millicent. That was the second Suzie.

And she realized she was now being the third Suzie and trying to talk like the Select Seven and making everything she told sound like a radio serial. Of course her mother thought she was whining and feeling sorry for herself, but you *couldn't* tell her you wished she'd stop being a teacher and just be a regular mother.

Suzie dragged her feet across the kitchen and slammed a cupboard door. "I'm just sick and tired of being an only child—not only in this house but in the whole darned neighborhood. Oh, what's the use? Not one single soul understands!"

Suzie's mother said, "Suzie, I've been thinking about your May poster. Why don't you paint one that would show a new child, like Co Co, how much fun an American school really is?"

Instantly Suzie stopped glowering and shuffling her feet. She threw her arms around her mother. "Gosh, I'm glad you're a teacher. You always have the neatest ideas! Oh, I left my paints down in the Lookout. Would you have time to walk down with me and get them? Then I could do some sketches while you are at the meeting. Oh, Mother, you're the neatest mother in the world!"

Suzie's mother shook her head. "Suzie, you are what is known as a mercurial character. We'll have to hurry because it's almost eight o'clock."

As Suzie skipped along beside her mother, the blossoming trees were milky in the twilight, the light on the mountain peaks was a filmy pink, and the sailboats were like little white triangles of paper on the darkening lake. "Oh, what a beautiful evening," she sang as she climbed up into the Lookout, collected her paints and her big drawing tablet, and started down the ladder.

She looked down on the Pink House and her heart came up in her throat. No longer did it lie like a wrapped Christmas package under the trees waiting to be opened. Tonight lights shone invitingly from the doorway, the house was bathed in the same delicate pink glow as the mountains, the pool gleamed like a blue turquoise, the gardens were shadowed, and night birds called softly to one another in the opalescent twilight.

Suzie called down, "Mother, I can hardly believe it. The people in the Pink House are *real*!"

Chapter Two

A French Friend

During school the next morning, Suzie was so happy that Miss Morrison had to remind her several times to pay attention. No matter how hard she tried to keep her mind on her lessons, she kept seeing Co Co's face and hearing her say, "Oui, Papa," and "Oui, Mademoiselle," and wondering if she would come to Maple Leaf and be in Miss Morrison's room.

Miss Morrison said, "Suzie, I must have your attention," and Millicent hissed, "Teacher's pet," but instead of blushing and hanging her head, Suzie smiled at Miss Morrison and Millicent, and said, "I'm sorry. I was thinking about something else."

On the playground after lunch, Rich and Ray were coaching Suzie to improve her pitching arm. Ray explained, "That's good, but if you want to pitch a curve, you've gotta hold the ball like this, see?"

Millicent walked over, followed by the Select Seven and said, "Fourteen looks like the cat that swallowed the canary. She wouldn't be so smart if she knew that five asked me for a date." She pointed at Suzie and they all whispered and giggled. Instantly the Pink House secret began to buzz around inside of Suzie like a bee in a jar. She almost opened her mouth and let the secret out, but Ray said, "Shut up, Millicent. Suzie, you're the only girl who can pitch, but you've gotta wind up first like this, see?" He wound up and threw the ball clear out of the playground.

While Ray was getting the ball, Rich continued, "But dear Millicent throws underhand, like this." He danced up to Millicent and tossed the ball right under her nose. She screamed and threatened to tell Miss Morrison whereupon Rich, in a squeaky imitation of her bossy voice said, "Oh, girls, I almost forgot— five plus two equals Seven Sickly Saps." All the boys laughed and slapped their thighs, the girls giggled, and Millicent flounced off to tattle.

All afternoon Millicent whispered in code and called Suzie "teacher's pet," but Suzie found she didn't even care, and for the first time began to think that perhaps Millicent wasn't so important after all.

The moment school was dismissed, Suzie grabbed her books and ran all the way home. She burst in the kitchen door, and gasped, "Grandmother, did anything new happen? Could you see what they were doing? Did you see Co Co?"

Grandmother said, "Trucks going back and forth all day long. I'll admit I am so curious I almost climbed up into the Lookout, but Bill Langdon might think it a little odd if he found me crouching in a tree at my age. Oh, yes, I have something for you."

Suzie danced up and down with impatience while Grandmother picked Snowball, her white kitten, off her shoulder and set him down among the red geraniums on the window sill, with, "There, now—you can play jungle." She brushed Marigold, her yellow cat, off her lap, with, "Pardon me, but I have to stand up." She stepped carefully around Smokey, her gray cat, who was winding around her legs and purring, with, "I trust you are not telling me you are going to have kittens again," and finally reached behind her and handed Suzie a small picnic basket covered with a red checked napkin. "See if that's enough. I put in two bottles of orangeade, two straws, two apples, and four ginger cookies."

"Enough for what?" Suzie asked.

"Enough for you and Co Co. It always seems so much easier to get acquainted with strangers when you are both eating something. Now skip up and change your clothes and for goodness sake, remember everything that happens so you can tell me."

"Oh, Grandmother, you're so neat!" Suzie hugged

her grandmother and flew up the back stairs. She jerked on jeans and a T-shirt, rushed downstairs, and grabbed the basket, blew a kiss, whistled to Jet, and ran as fast as she could go to the Lookout.

She climbed up the ladder and there, sitting cross-legged on the floor and reading a book, was Co Co.

Suzie blushed and said all in one breath, "Hello, I'm Suzie Green and this is Jet, our dog, and I'm so glad you're going to move in."

Co Co nodded. "Bonjour, Suzie. Bonjour, Jet. I am delighted to meet you. I regret if I intrude. I climbed on the platform to see the mountains and the lake. We see all of America from here. Do we not?"

"Oh gosh, no! This is just a little part of western Washington. Grandmother fixed us a picnic. Would you like some?"

Co Co's face broke into a delighted smile. "Indeed, yes. With pleasure. I am always hungry. We live at the hotel until our house is ready." She spread her hands. "It is horrible! So dark, so ugly!"

While Suzie divided the picnic, Co Co kept up a steady stream of questions about America. Some of her words were in French, but Suzie found that if she listened carefully, she understood what Co Co meant without any difficulty. Co Co gestured constantly with her hands, and when she was hunting for an English word, she paused, shrugged, and held her head on one side like a robin listening for a worm.

Co Co's face reminded Suzie of a Flemish painting she had seen at the art museum. Her eyebrows were like charcoal strokes that tilted up at the corners, her large dark eyes were shadowed with straight dark lashes, she had a wide mouth, a pointed chin with a dimple in the center, and freckles across the bridge of her nose like a sprinkling of black pepper.

To keep from staring and being rude, Suzie asked, "Have you always gone to a French school?"

"Oh, mais non! I have never attended school. I have had a—a governess—who supervised my education. Tell me, Suzie, do American girls wear—uh—the pants?" She pointed to Suzie's jeans.

"Sure. We always wear them after school and on Saturdays. Don't you?"

Co Co threw up her hands. "Mademoiselle would not approve. Not at all. In France well-brought-up young ladies do not wear the pants. But now that I am in America, I, too, will wear them. It is well that you live so near to me. That is your house there, in the trees, is it not?"

Suzie nodded and swallowed to give her nerve enough to ask the all-important question. "Co Co, how old are you? Not that it makes one bit of difference, I don't care really, but I just wanted to know."

Co Co said, "I have eleven years. And you?"

"I'm eleven, too. I will be twelve on July first."

Co Co clapped her hands. "I, too, will have twelve years July three. So, we are the same age. Excellent! Are you also as tall as me? Let us stand."

They stood back to back while Suzie rested a book on the top of their heads. It balanced perfectly.

They grinned at one another and sat down again. Jet obligingly made room for both of them to lean against him. Co Co said, "I did not know a dog would also make a chair. He is comfortable, are you not, Jet?" She patted him and murmured French endearments, which he seemed to enjoy.

"Did you always speak French before you came here?" Suzie asked.

"Yes, with Mademoiselle and the other French people. Papa usually speaks English with me. I speak both of them. With you I will speak both of them together. Suzie, is there another little cake in that basket?" She fished around until she found the last two cookies, offered one to Suzie who refused, and ate both of them with great relish.

"Have you always lived in France, Co Co?"

"I think you would say we lived in Paris, but Papa is an engineer and we traveled constantly. We lived in Italy, England, Sweden, Holland, and once in Spain and in Egypt. It was tiresome and sometimes so dirty!"

"How neat!" Suzie's eyes were shining. "I've always wanted to travel."

Co Co shrugged. "It is pleasant to be with Papa, but it is also tiresome. We fly all the time and the airplane makes me sick."

"I've always wanted to fly. Is it fun to live in France?"

"Mais oui. All of France is beautiful, but you would love Paris. The puppets and the theaters and the flowers and the parks and the little sidewalk cafes. Paris is so beautiful!"

Suzie sighed blissfully. "If only social studies were like this."

Co Co said, "And what is that—social studies?"

"Oh, geography and history and government and principal cities and rivers and imports and stuff, and it's so dull! Promise you won't laugh at me if I tell you something?"

Co Co shook her head. "I will not laugh."

"I've never even been on a train or a plane."

"Oh, you are indeed fortunate. You have traveled by boat, perhaps?"

"Not even by boat. I've never been *anywhere*. I've stayed right here all my life in this very same house."

"You are indeed fortunate. To live in a house instead of hotels and be with other children. I would like that."

Suzie was so astonished she leaned over and peered

into Co Co's face to see if she was teasing, but Co Co looked serious and wistful.

"Oh, Suzie, I have never been in one city long enough to have a dear friend of my age. Always, except for Mademoiselle and Papa and the children in the hotels, I have been alone. But now, Papa has promised me I will not travel and I may attend school. Is that not wonderful?"

Again Suzie leaned over to see if Co Co was teasing, and again her face was wistful. "My gosh, that's the first time I ever heard school called wonderful. Why, in my room . . ." Suzie began her long tale about school and Millicent and the Select Seven and Rich and Ray and Miss Morrison.

Co Co listened as if it were the most fascinating story she had ever heard. Occasionally she interrupted to ask the meaning of a word, but mostly to say over and over again, "Tell me more—tell me more."

Co Co was so understanding that for the first time in her life, Suzie found her real thoughts just tumbling out. How awful it was to have your mother a teacher; how scared she was in school; how much she hated to be called "teacher's pet"; all the things she had kept bottled up inside of her.

Co Co nodded sympathetically. "I know, the children at the hotel thought I did not study because I did not attend the school. I had to study all the time—all the t me. The only time Mademoiselle does not teach me is when she is asleep!"

Suzie cheered up so much she began to tell Co Co all the pleasant things she could think of about school. Miss Morrison was just neat, and Rich and Ray were so funny they were just neat, and Marjorie and Sumiko and Barbara were keen girls, they were just neat.

Co Co interrupted her. "This word 'neat'—does it not mean orderly?"

"It does, but when you speak American, you don't use hardly any words at all. Anything that's good—I mean really just neat—well, you say 'neat' or 'keen' and if something is really gruesome, you say 'grubby' or 'droopy' or 'ghastly.' It's a lot easier."

Co Co nodded. "I will remember that. Mademoiselle will not approve but . . ."

Just then they heard Mademoiselle calling, "Clothilde? Clothilde? Clothilde?"

"Do you see?" Co Co made a face and leaned over the edge of the platform and called, "Je viens, Mademoiselle." She started down the ladder and then peered over the edge of the platform and put her finger to her lips. "Mademoiselle will not care for the tree house. We will not speak of it for the present." She giggled and disappeared.

Suzie watched her run across the garden, curtsy to Mademoiselle, heard her speaking rapid French and then watched Mademoiselle shake her head and frown and use her scolding voice. "Non, Clothilde, non, non."

Co Co stamped her foot and waggled her fingers behind her back at Suzie and continued to argue in French with Mademoiselle. Finally with a last "Non, Clothilde, non, non," Mademoiselle shrugged and turned and walked into the house.

Co Co made a hideous face toward Mademoiselle's retreating back and blew a kiss toward the Lookout. Then her father came out the door and said, "What's all this, Co Co? What's all the fuss about?"

"It is Suzie, Papa. She is not a stranger. She is the daughter of your friends. She lives in the trees there. Mademoiselle forbids me to talk with her. I will not—I will not—" She began waving her arms toward the Lookout and speaking rapid French and stamping her foot until Suzie was worried for fear her father would not let her come back.

Co Co's father said quietly, "Calm down, Co Co. Gently—gently. You may play with Suzie. She must be the Wellses' granddaughter. Please ask her to give my fondest regards to her family and tell her that I will call on them soon."

Co Co beamed. "Merci, Papa, merci, merci. I will go and tell Suzie." Like a flash she ran across the patio and up the ladder. "My papa wishes to send his regards to your family. Mademoiselle cannot tell me what to do now. I am an American. Tell me more about that marvelous school."

"Okay. But first tell me something. Is Mademoiselle your mother or your aunt or something?" Co Co laughed. "Oh, mais non. She is my governess. My mother died when I was little." She reached down inside of her blouse, pulled out a locket, and opened it. "Here is a picture of my mother."

Suzie saw a beautiful young girl's face, very much like Co Co's with the same dimpled chin and tilted eyebrows. "My mother was also called Clothilde, but she was very beautiful." Co Co put the locket back and sighed.

Suzie said, "I know just how you feel. My father was in the navy and was drowned when I was two years old. I'll show you his picture when we go to my house."

Co Co patted Suzie comfortingly. "The war. So terrible! My father was also gone for a long, long time. But Suzie, I have thought of something. A moment— no, I do not know the English word. When two children are born the same day, from the same mother, what do you say?"

Suzie thought a moment. "Oh, do you mean when they're twins?"

"Oui, oui," Co Co grinned. "Violà. We are almost twins, are we not?"

Suddenly a commotion in the patio below interrupted them. They leaned over and watched Mademoiselle obviously arguing with Co Co's father. She gestured toward the Lookout, waved her hands and shook her head. Co Co's father's calm words were like English commas in Mademoiselle's angry French. "Nonsense, yes, yes, I know it, ridiculous, I gave her permission, nonsense." But instead of calming down, Mademoiselle became more and more excited.

Co Co chuckled. "Ha-ha—Mademoiselle is now scolding Papa."

They burst out laughing and giggled until their stomachs were sore. Finally Co Co gasped, "Oh, my Suzie, it is indeed marvelous to laugh. Oh, I am so happy. Now tell me more about the marvelous school."

Suzie promptly launched into her radio serial version of how mean everyone was to her and how awful Rich and Ray were to Miss Morrison and on and on. But to her astonishment, Co Co, instead of sympathizing, ended each harrowing story with, "Oh, c'est formidable!" which so obviously meant "keen" and "neat" that Suzie began to wonder if school was so awful after all.

Co Co even clasped her arms around her knees and rocked back and forth and demanded more and more tales of Millicent's behavior. "This Millicent, what a bad girl! Tell me, Suzie, how does this school appear?"

"Here, I'll show you." Suzie unlocked one of her cupboards and took out several sketches of Maple Leaf. She explained the pictures of the large red brick school and showed Co Co where her room was. Each window held spring flowers, children formed rings around Maypoles, children were square dancing in old-fashioned costumes, teachers were standing and smiling beside each ring of children. Suzie had used watercolors in some and colored pencils in others and Co Co was delighted.

"Maple Leaf is indeed formidable! The pictures, they are excellent. You are indeed an artist, my Suzie, and I would love to see this school."

"I know what I'll do. I'll ask Mother if it would be all right for you to go to school with me. Mother teaches the fourth grade and Miss Morrison is our teacher. Guess what Miss Morrison is going to do? She is going to marry an old principal!"

"And what is that—an old principal?"

"He's just head of the whole school, that's all. Mr. Wagner, the principal of our school, is so different from most. He is very strict of course, he has to be, but he's really just neat! He lets us visit factories and the jail and fire stations and everything and we have programs on all the school holidays and we go to symphonies."

"But do you not study arithmetic and grammar and history?"

"Oh sure, but that's the dull part."

Co Co demanded all the stories about Millicent and the Select Seven over again. They talked and giggled until Co Co's father's head appeared over the edge of the platform. "This is a dandy tree house. Ours was right here, too, but it wasn't half this good. Suzie, I'm awfully glad to see you. Grandmother Wells says we just have time to take you on a tour of our house, and then we are to come straight home for dinner." He laughed, a deeper and more rumbling version of Co Co's chuckle. "And if I remember correctly and I certainly do, our hands had better be clean and we'd better not be late. I have driven Mademoiselle back to the hotel, and I need some advice about the house."

As they climbed down and walked across the patio, Suzie was so excited she could hardly speak. At last, she was going to see the inside of the Pink House! By the time Co Co's father opened the front door, her heart was beating so hard she was almost dizzy.

But when she walked into the hall she nearly cried out with disappointment. It wasn't light and airy and beautiful. It was dark and gloomy with brown woodwork and stucco walls. The living room was cold and stiff and reminded her of an aquarium with its dull green walls and thin gold chairs. She almost jumped when she saw the big black piano, its keys like bared teeth, crouched in one corner. The dining room was even gloomier, with cross-looking portraits scowling from the walls. The kitchen was white tiled and reminded her of the dentist, and the bedrooms looked cold and unlived in. It was so depressing that Suzie said, "Grandmother's kitchen is the nicest place in our house. She has a rocking chair and geraniums on the window sills and it looks sunshiny. . . ." She clapped her hands over her mouth for fear she had hurt Co Co and her father's feelings.

Co Co's father ruffled Suzie's hair. "And at least four cats and a dog and it always smells of cookies when you come home from school. . . ."

And Co Co said, "Perhaps your grand'mère would help us."

Suzie was so relieved that Co Co wasn't going to live in this dark mournful place that she said quickly, "Oh, she would. And we have bowls of flowers and books and magazines and Grandfather's pipes. . . ."

"And it's the most comfortable house I've ever been in," Co Co's father added. "We'll make this one just as comfortable, so don't worry. Now, we'd better go because it's almost five-thirty."

When they reached the orchard, he said, "Here— each of you take a hand and I'll show you the shortest way home." Suzie and Co Co barely touched the ground as he jumped the hedge and took giant steps. Jet barked and ran back and forth and they arrived at the back door breathless with laughter.

Grandmother opened the door. "Bill Langdon, you have no more sense of time than a cricket." She reached up and kissed him. Then she put her arms around Co Co and said, "Welcome home, my dear."

Grandfather greeted Mr. Langdon as if he were a part of the family, and Suzie's mother blushed when he said, "I'm sorry I ever called you 'pest.'"

As Suzie watched all this kissing and welcoming, she wondered if Grandmother had forgotten that just last night she was kind of mad at Mr. Langdon.

"Come on in the living room," Suzie's mother said. "I'm dying to know what you've been doing all these years."

Grandmother turned to Co Co, just as if she'd known her all her life, and said, "Now you help Suzie set the table. Dinner is almost ready and I'm hungry as a bear."

Co Co smiled. "The bear is an animal. Hungry as a bear—I like that!"

While the grown people were in the living room talking about all the years Mr. Langdon had been away, Co Co and Suzie talked about America and Co Co's house and how they could make it more cheerful. While Suzie mashed the strawberries for the ice cream and toasted the angel food cake and made the salad, Co Co followed her around exclaiming, "But Suzie—you are so intelligent! You are a chef! You are so capable!" By the time dinner was ready, Suzie was so proud she was almost bursting.

During dinner Mr. Langdon entertained them with stories of their life in France and of the many places they had visited. The tales he told were more exciting than any movie Suzie had ever seen, and she listened so hard she forgot to swallow.

He said that after his wife had died he had been very unhappy and had written none of his old friends in America. Also that he had traveled a good deal of the time and had found it difficult to receive his personal mail. He went on, "You probably thought it strange my not writing to what I have always considered my own family." He patted Grandmother's hand. "But I knew you'd understand if I ever got back. I knew our house would be waiting for us, and now that we are going to live in America, Co Co will be going to school here, and Mademoiselle can go back to Paris and resume her teaching there."

Suzie swallowed, "But if Mademoiselle goes back to Paris, who will take care of Co Co? She could come and live with us—I have twin beds in my room."

Mr. Langdon smiled. "I expect Co Co will spend most of her time here, just as I did. However, Mrs. MacGregor, the daughter of Mother's housekeeper, is going to keep house for us. She has even offered to stay during the remodeling to see that everything goes well."

Meanwhile Co Co, who was calmly eating her third serving of fried chicken and spoon bread and green peas, murmured, "But this is delicious. American food is so delicious."

About ten o'clock, after Suzie had taken Co Co over every inch of her house, and Co Co had decided to make their house exactly like it even to the four cats, Mr. Langdon said it was time for them to go back to the hotel or Mademoiselle would scold them.

Co Co curtsied to the grown-ups and said, "Bonsoir, dear friends of my father, thank you for a delightful evening." Then she motioned to Suzie and led her over to the corner of the hall, out of earshot of the grown people.

"Suzie, have you une chère amie—a dear friend?" she asked.

Suzie said, "Well no, that's just the trouble. I've never had a best friend."

Co Co took Suzie's face tenderly in her hands and kissed her on either cheek. "Good! I will be your best friend, my dear Suzie."

Chapter Three

Saturday

Saturday had always been Suzie's favorite day of the week, for it was the only day she could depend upon to have her mother's undivided attention. If it was sunshiny, they did housework and worked in the garden until lunchtime. If it was raining, they went shopping, had lunch downtown, and spent the afternoon exploring.

Sometimes they went to the museums or to the zoo. Sometimes they just took a bus and rode to the end of the line. The bus trips were fun because they found fishing fleets and lumber mills, and once they found a glass blower and a lady who raised lovebirds. Suzie could never make up her mind whether she liked the rainy or the sunny Saturdays best.

On this Saturday morning, however, Suzie was so excited about Co Co that she couldn't concentrate on her chores and kept following her mother around asking questions about the Langdons. Most of the things her mother told her she already knew as well as she knew the days of the week—the Langdons and the Wellses were pioneer families—they had bought adjoining farms when Seattle was still a village. Bill Langdon was an only child who had spent most of his time at the Wellses' house because he was lonely.

Suzie kept asking questions until her mother finally said, "I've really told you all I know about the Langdons. Now hurry, darling."

Suzie peered around a dishtowel she was hanging on the line. "Didn't Mr. Langdon even write and tell you Co Co was born?" She watched her mother's face carefully as she asked this question.

Suzie's mother said, "No darling, and there was really no reason why he should. When grown people do not see each other for a long time, they don't always write letters."

"But Mother, you said he was just like your brother."

Suzie's mother sighed. "If we're going to get the weeding done, we'd better get started."

Suzie picked up her basket of gardening tools and knelt down beside her flower bed. She planted a row of nasturtiums and thought about the Langdons. If Mr. Langdon went away and didn't write and hurt their feelings, then why did they act so glad to see him?

She sighed. "Sometimes I think I'll never understand grown people."

She looked over her seed packages and decided to plant a row of bachelor's buttons for Mr. Langdon. She was wondering if a man whose wife died turned into a bachelor again, when she was startled to hear, "Bonjour, my best friend. How are you this morning?"

She turned around and there was Co Co, wearing a new red plaid shirt, jeans, and loafers.

"Hi, Co Co. Your new outfit is neat. Where'd you get it?"

"I went to the shops this morning and said I wished to buy an American costume for play. It was a little difficult. I did not know all the words and the clerks did not seem to understand."

Suzie grinned as she remembered Co Co's confusing way of speaking half French and half English. She said, "You certainly did well. I wish I had a shirt like that."

Co Co handed her a package. "Ho-ho, but you have. I wished my twin to look like me."

Suzie ripped open the package and there was a blue plaid shirt just like Co Co's, and new studded jeans. "Co Co, how neat! Thank you ever so much."

"It is nothing. Papa said I could buy a present for my best friend." Co Co knelt down beside Suzie. "And what is it that we plant this morning?"

"Nasturtiums and bachelor's buttons, but let's go show my new outfit to Mother."

Suzie's mother exclaimed over the present and said, "Co Co, you are very chic this morning."

Co Co curtsied and then looked surprised. "These jeans—they do not make the curtsy."

Suzie's mother said, "Suzie, perhaps Co Co would like to have dinner with us tonight and go to a movie."

Co Co curtsied again and this time Suzie couldn't suppress a giggle. Co Co did look so strange, trying to hold out the sides of her jeans, as she said, "Merci, Madame, for the invitation and thank you also Suzie, but I am already engaged. Papa receives some guests this evening and Mademoiselle would not excuse me. Perhaps another time I may accept your kind invitation."

Co Co stamped her foot as she heard Mademoiselle calling, "Clothilde? Clothilde? Venez ici! Clothilde? Clothilde?" She said, "Au revoir. Mademoiselle will scold if I do not come quickly." She curtsied and ran out of the garden.

All the time Suzie and her mother were shopping Suzie thought about Co Co. She asked anxiously, "Mother, if I took Co Co to school with me, do you think the Select Seven would make fun of her?"

Suzie's mother said she doubted it. Children were usually fascinated with a new child and made her the center of attention. She added, "And of course she'll have you there to protect her."

The idea of protecting Co Co made Suzie feel so warm in her heart that she even told her mother that sometimes she wished she was a regular mother and not a teacher and about how hard it was to be a good student and yet not turn into a "teacher's pet."

Her mother said she realized Suzie's problem, but now that she had Co Co to play with, she didn't think it would bother her so much.

"Gosh, Mother, having a best friend makes me feel good. I don't even care about Millicent and the Select Seven anymore."

They spent the afternoon at the museum seeing how many French pictures they could find and talking about all the countries Co Co had visited. "Boy! I'll bet I'll even like social studies now that the countries seem real and not just colored spots on the map," Suzie said.

At about six, Suzie's mother was putting on her hat and Suzie was hopping around the front hall saying, "Hurry *up*, Mother. You know perfectly well we'll miss the beginning and you know perfectly well you won't want to stay through the second feature. Hurry *up*, Mother—" when the doorbell rang. "Oh, Mother, don't answer it. You know perfectly well it will be one of your friends and you'll have to talk for ages and ages.

This is a pioneer movie and Miss Morrison practically told us to go. Oh, Mother . . ."

Suzie's mother opened the front door and there stood Co Co, dressed as she had been the first time Suzie saw her.

"Bonsoir. May I join you for dinner and the cinema? Mademoiselle does not approve of my asking for the invitation, but Papa says we are in America now and there is the difference. He says his guests will discuss engineering and in America, the gentlemen prefer not to have ladies present when they discuss business."

Meanwhile Suzie was looking Co Co over enviously. "Gosh, you look grown up. I wish I had shoes with heels."

And Co Co was looking Suzie over equally carefully. "Is that the costume you will wear for dinner and the cinema?"

"Sure. It's just a neighborhood movie. I always wear just a sweater and skirt and my school coat."

Co Co said, "Would it inconvenience you, Madame, if I stopped at the hotel for a moment? I must speak to Papa."

They stopped at the hotel and Co Co came back wearing a sweater and skirt, a brown tweed coat, and her new loafers. She said breathlessly, "I hope I did not delay you, but Mademoiselle says it is courteous to dress in the fashion of the country in which one lives. I am so excited! This is my first American engagement."

"We'll make it as American as possible then," Suzie's mother said as they drove to a drive-in restaurant.

When the waitress came out to get their orders, she handed each of them a menu and said, "What'll it be, folks? I'll be back in a jiffy."

Co Co grinned. "We are folks then." She giggled. "I like that word 'jeefy.' I will remember him." She read the menu for a long time and Suzie could hear her reading under her breath "'amburger," "cheeseburger," "'ot dog," "jumbo 'amburger." Finally she sighed and shook her head. "I am afraid I do not know these words. I believe you must order the dinner for me."

Suzie's mother ordered three jumbo hamburgers, three green salads, and three chocolate ice cream sodas. When the waitress brought the trays and hooked them to the doors of the car, she said, "There now. Everything okey-dokey?" Co Co chuckled and answered, "Everything is indeed okey-dokey, merci beaucoup," at which the waitress looked so surprised that Suzie giggled.

Co Co was enchanted with the drive-in. She watched Suzie unwrap the top of her hamburger and take an enormous bite. Then she picked up her own hamburger and peered inside of it. "A little roll with meat in the middle. C'est formidable!" She watched Suzie unwrap her straws and take a drink of her soda, but when she also took a big swallow, she sneezed. "It tickles my nose, but is delicious." She took another swallow and made such loud gargling sounds that they both giggled helplessly.

Finally Suzie's mother announced they'd better get started or she wouldn't guarantee that she wouldn't fall asleep during the second feature. They started north on the highway and Suzie said, "Mother, where on earth are you going? This isn't the way to the movie."

Suzie's mother smiled. "Wait and see. Curiosity killed the cat, remember."

Co Co said, "It killed the cat of my father also. He says that when I ask questions."

When they came to a high board fence and Suzie's mother turned the car into a drive-in theater, Suzie was delighted. "Oh goodie! I've never been to one of these, and I've always wanted to go. And they've got the very same pioneer movie. How neat!"

Suzie's mother bought them each a bag of popcorn and they settled back comfortably in the car. The pioneer movie was in color with lots of shooting and riding. Again Suzie heard Co Co translating under her breath, so she asked, "How do you say 'chuck-wagon' in French?"

Co Co said quickly, "Sh, or I will lose myself."

The second feature was a mystery which had so much sneaking through dark buildings and so many careening cars, that Co Co had no difficulty following the action.

When the cartoon came on, Co Co watched it for a few moments and then exclaimed, "But we have these little animals in Paris also, but they speak French! How quick they are and how intelligent to speak English here."

It was almost twelve o'clock when they stopped in front of the hotel. The doorman opened the door and said, "Good evening. Good evening Mademoiselle Co Co. Did you enjoy your first American evening?"

Co Co said, "Oh, Henri, it was delightful and very, very American. It was okey-dokey!"

Chapter Four

Co Co Attends the School

Monday morning Suzie came down early and prowled around the kitchen muttering, "Grandmother, what if Co Co is late? Yes, but what if she doesn't know how awful it is if you're late? Yes, but I've never been tardy. Yes, but what if they make fun of her accent? Oh, I do wish she'd hurry."

Finally Grandmother said, "Sit down, Suzie, and drink your orange juice and Co Co will be here before you can say Jack Robinson."

Before Grandmother even finished saying "Robinson," a taxi stopped in front of the house, Co Co got out, paid the driver, and came running around to the back door. Suzie opened the door. "Gosh! I was so worried. I thought you'd be late!"

Co Co was excited. "Bonjour, Grand'mère. Suzie, I do not sleep. I toss on the bed. I do not close my eyes.

I get up at six o'clock with the birds to dress. Is this the correct costume?"

Grandmother assured her, "You look as fresh and crisp as if you'd just been lifted out of a bandbox."

Suzie chimed in, "Our outfits are just the same except your sweater's red and mine's green. I was so worried. I thought you'd never come."

Grandmother said, "Now calm down, both of you. Have you had breakfast, Co Co?"

"Non, Grand'mère. I had café au lait and a little roll at the hotel, but it did not rest on my stomach."

Suzie gasped, "Is that coffee? Does your father allow you to drink *coffee*?"

"Well, it is hot milk with a little coffee in it. In France they also drink chocolate, but I do not care for it."

"We have to drink plain milk even if we just hate it."

Co Co sat down and sipped her glass of milk. "It is not too disagreeable, but I am not accustomed to it. It is so cold. I believe I prefer café au lait."

Grandmother clucked disapprovingly but she fixed Co Co a cup of warm milk with a little coffee in it. Suzie tasted it and promptly demanded some also.

Then Grandmother gave them plates piled high with scrambled eggs, crisp bacon, and hot muffins. "Now, eat every bit of that and your stomachs will stop jumping. I declare, you'd think this was the first time either one of you had been to school."

While they were eating, Co Co asked Suzie over and over again about school. By the time they'd finished breakfast they were both in such a state of nerves, Grandmother suggested that they start early and give themselves plenty of time to look the school over before classes began.

As they walked up the street, Suzie told Co Co all about the people who lived in each house, and pointed out the dogs that were friendly and the ones who barked even if they didn't mean it. "This is your neighborhood now, and you should know everything about everybody."

Co Co squeezed Suzie's hand. "Oui, Suzie, this is my first neighborhood."

When they passed the Tower House where Mrs. Medlin lived, Suzie warned Co Co never to climb her trees, or pick her fruit, or even to *touch* anything in her yard. "She's just about the crabbiest lady in Seattle. She acts just as if she *hates* children and dogs."

Co Co peeked over the fence. Mrs. Medlin was kneeling with her back to them, weeding. Without even turning around, she roared, "Children, don't you dare take the shortcut through my garden!"

Co Co jumped back and Suzie giggled. "See? Boy, she's crabby! She lives all alone—probably because nobody would dare live with her."

When they arrived at the school grounds, Co Co

hung back and her eyes were wide with fright. Pushing, giggling children streamed up the steps and poured out onto the playground, calling to one another with early morning shouts of joy. She listened to all the noise and murmured, "Oh, Suzie, my stomach! I do not think I can attend the school."

Suzie took her hand and said, in a loud brave voice, "Oh, come on. You'll just love it." Her own heart always pounded and her hands shook when she walked through the crowd of shouting, pushing children, but if she was going to protect Co Co, she couldn't let her know how she felt, so she waved and called, "Hi" right and left. She led Co Co over to the big willow tree. "We'll sit here until the bell rings, and I'll show you who everybody is."

Co Co, her eyes wide and black as she watched the crowds of noisy children, pressed close to Suzie. "But there are so many. I did not know there were so many."

Rich and Ray came tearing by, stopped, eyed Co Co for a moment, then Rich said, "Hi, Suze, old girl. Want to play catch?"

"Thanks. I can't now," Suzie answered. "I'll see you at recess."

The boys walked off and stood at a little distance, still eyeing Co Co.

Suzie whispered, "That's Rich and Ray, the twins I was telling you about. They're good athletes and smart in school, but they tease Miss Morrison. Sometimes she can't tell them apart and . . ."

Just then the Select Seven, their arms entwined, sauntered toward them. Suzie heard, "Four likes six." And "Did he really call you?" And "His mother wouldn't even call him to the phone. I nearly died." They, too, eyed Co Co, but instead of stopping they went whispering and giggling on.

Suzie said, "They are the Select Seven. They never speak to anybody. They have a number code, so they never call people by their names—just numbers. They are really nice girls except they're awfully boy crazy." She sighed.

"What is that—boy crazy?" Co Co asked.

"Oh, you know—they like boys—they're kind of in love."

"Non!" Co Co gasped. "They are children! They are too young for—what you say—the boy crazy!" Then, in Mademoiselle's most haughty manner, she added, "I do not approve of that!"

With Millicent in the lead, the Select Seven paraded back and forth talking in code for the benefit of Suzie's new friend. Suzie called to them, but they didn't answer and Suzie was so embarrassed she said, "Just pretend you don't see them."

Co Co shuddered. "I do not care. I am so frightened. Tell me about the school again."

Feeling more and more protective, Suzie put her arm around Co Co and said that first the bell rang and then they had roll call, and then language arts. Co Co looked so bewildered that Suzie added, "You remember. That's English and spelling and reading and grammar."

Co Co swallowed. "Papa says if one has studied Latin—the English sentence is not too difficult."

"Gosh! Have you had Latin already?"

"Oh yes, but I do not read it well. The English verbs. Impossible! Oh, I know I will appear stupid and Mademoiselle will be ashamed." Co Co wrung her hands.

Suzie patted her comfortingly. "You'll be terrific in social studies, and then we have arithmetic. That's my favorite next to art and music."

Co Co groaned. "I cannot do arithmetic in English!" She rested her chin in her hands and muttered to herself in French as she stared at the playground, which was alive with brightly dressed boys and girls playing catch, roller skating on the cement court, jumping rope, bouncing balls, playing jacks and marbles, and just tearing around and yelling and screaming. Suzie could barely hear Co Co saying over and over again, "I did not think there were this many children in all of America."

The bell rang and the shouting children promptly

quieted down and melted into lines and began to stream into the school. Suzie stood up and took Co Co's hand. "Come on—that's the first bell and we can go into Mr. Wagner's office now."

She led Co Co into the reception room. While they were waiting for Mr. Wagner, Co Co watched the schoolroom doors opening and closing, listened to all the busy school sounds, the running feet, the bells, the whispering, and became more bewildered than ever. "This school is so large. I cannot attend this school. I will go back to the hotel and ask Papa if Mademoiselle cannot stay and teach me." She got up and started out the door.

Suzie grabbed her just as Mr. Wagner came out of his office. Before this moment, Suzie had been so in awe of Mr. Wagner that she spoke just above a whisper. Knowing that Co Co was depending on her, she said in a loud, sure voice, "Good morning, Mr. Wagner. This is my friend Co Co Langdon, the new girl mother called you about."

Co Co peeked out from behind Suzie and whispered, "Bonjour, Monsieur," and curtsied.

Mr. Wagner said, "Suzie, I'm glad to see you. Good morning, Clothilde, I hope you will allow us to call you Co Co, also."

Co Co nodded and whispered, "Oui, Monsieur." They followed Mr. Wagner into his office and Co Co murmured, "Oh, Suzie, my English—it is leaving me." She put an ice cold hand in Suzie's and hung back.

Mr. Wagner took some forms from his desk drawer and began to fill them out. He talked quietly, asked Co Co a great many questions, and didn't seem to notice that most of her replies were in French. When he was through, he explained the school rules and schedule. Co Co nodded, but she still appeared so confused that Suzie asked, "Mr. Wagner, could you take a tour of the school with us? Mother says that makes a new child feel less strange."

Suzie crossed her fingers in her lap because her mother hadn't said that at all, but she knew the Select Seven wouldn't dare be rude and make fun of Co Co if Mr. Wagner was standing right there.

As they walked through the halls, Mr. Wagner was so kind and friendly that Co Co was soon chattering away—part in English and part in French, just as if she were talking to Suzie.

Meanwhile Suzie was watching Mr. Wagner and trying to think of him as Miss Morrison's date. He was really quite handsome, but it was hard to imagine anybody thirty years old having a date.

Mr. Wagner stopped in front of Miss Morrison's room. "And this is Suzie's room, where you will be. It might help you to remember that every once in a while one of our pupils goes to France to live. It is more difficult for them than it will be for you, because they do not have the advantage of knowing two languages. Miss Morrison is an especially good teacher, isn't she, Suzie?" He winked and opened the door and led them up to Miss Morrison's desk.

"Miss Morrison, children, this is Co Co Langdon. I am sure you will be especially courteous to her because she is not only new to the school, she is new to the country as well. Good-bye, Co Co, and good luck. Be sure to come to me if you have any further questions."

Miss Morrison smiled and said, "Good morning, Co Co. Suzie's mother has told me all about you. We are especially glad to have you in our room, because you are the first French child we have had the privilege of knowing."

There was a gasp from the class as Co Co curtsied and said, "Bonjour, Mademoiselle Morrison." There was a loud "Ohhhh!" when Miss Morrison said something to Co Co in French. Whereupon Co Co's face lighted up and she cascaded a torrent of French, gesturing with both hands as she spoke.

Miss Morrison turned to the churning, whispering class. "This morning we have a very exciting new pupil, Clothilde Langdon. Her friends call her Co Co. She is an American who has always lived in France, and I know you will be especially courteous to her." She led Co Co to a seat across from Suzie.

Millicent turned and stared at her.

Co Co said, "Pardonnez moi, Mademoiselle Morrison. I have lived in France more than any other country, but I have traveled so much." Her voice dropped and she blushed. "That I have never attended school." She sat down and folded her hands.

There were whispers from all over the room and round-eyed stares as Miss Morrison introduced each of the children. "This is Johnny Allen, Co Co. Johnny is excellent in arithmetic and our best football player." Johnny mumbled "Hi" and watched Co Co from under his lashes. "And these are Rich and Ray Clark. They are twins as you see, and they are famous for their experiments—particularly the one where they try to confuse me so I can't tell them apart." She put her arm around a lovely little girl with black hair and bangs. "This is Sumiko Ito, who draws so beautifully. She, too, is an American who has spent most of her life in another country. Until last year Sumiko went to school in Japan."

As Miss Morrison moved up and down the aisles, saying something kind about everyone, Suzie didn't blame Mr. Wagner for wanting to marry her. She was so pretty and so neat and she always made everyone feel proud.

When Miss Morrison finished the introductions, she said she thought it would be fun, instead of having language arts, to spend the first period entertaining Co Co. "Let's start with 'The Plaint of the Camel' by Charles Carryl. Suzie, you may say the verse and we will all join in the chorus."

Co Co sat perfectly still with folded hands and downcast eyes and Suzie felt so sorry for her, that instead of blushing and stammering as she usually did when she had to recite, she marched right up in front of the room and with a smile began: "Cats you're aware, can repose in a chair . . ." All during the verse she fixed her eyes on Co Co, and when the class shouted, "Any load does for me," Co Co finally smiled.

When Suzie finished there was almost a breeze from the frantically waving hands. Miss Morrison said they wouldn't have time for everybody, so perhaps it would be best if they each said one verse of his favorite poem. When it was Millicent's turn, she simpered, "I'd like to say 'Little Orphant Annie.'" She used such baby talk and made so many gestures that Co Co couldn't understand her.

Rich said, "Boy, are you corny!" Ray pretended to gag, and Millicent tossed her head and twitched her skirts and sat down.

Rich said, "Miss Morrison, Ray and I know a special poem we'd like to say for Co Co." Miss Morrison nodded and they walked to the front of the room, grinned at Co Co, and bowed formally to one another.

Ray began, "My dear Gaston, you may call a woman a kitten."

Rich continued, "My dear Alphonse, but you must not call her a cat."

They alternated with mouse and rat, chicken and hen, duck and goose.

When they had finished, Co Co laughed hardest of all and said out loud, "You see, my Suzie, English is a bizarre language."

Millicent turned around. "Of all the nerve—talking right out loud in school."

Co Co blushed and again sat with downcast eyes and folded hands.

Suzie muttered, "You shut up, Millicent!" and Millicent waved her hand to tattle, but Miss Morrison ignored her and told the class to get out their arithmetic books. When she finished putting the assignment on the board, Suzie was horrified to see two large tears on Co Co's cheeks. She whispered, "Don't worry. I'll help you," but Co Co just shook her head and wound her hands together.

Miss Morrison came and sat beside Co Co and pointed to a page of problems in the book. "We'll have to see how much arithmetic you have had. Can you do these problems?"

"Oui, Mademoiselle." Co Co did them neatly and rapidly.

Miss Morrison said, "Excellent!" She turned to another page. "Can you do these also?"

"Oui, Mademoiselle." Co Co also did the fractions.

Suzie, who was leaning over and watching, noticed that although her long division looked strange, the answers were right.

Miss Morrison said, "You'll have no difficulty at all. Is there anything you would like to have me help you with?"

Co Co nodded and turned over the pages until she came to some word problems about Henry building a fence. She swallowed. "Mademoiselle Morrison, I cannot help Henry. If he wishes a fence he must take his own measures in meters."

Miss Morrison laughed. "It might be a little difficult to help Henry at first, but that will come. You do what you can, and I'll help you with the rest. Your arithmetic is excellent."

Co Co sighed and began to copy the problems on the board. Suzie checked her paper when she was through, and although her problems looked peculiar, every single one of them was right.

The bell rang and Suzie said, "Come on, it's time for physical education. We'll play baseball and it's loads of fun."

With misgivings, Suzie introduced Co Co to Miss Wright, the gymnasium teacher. Miss Wright was neat, but she did slap you on the back and talk loud, and her hearty manner might frighten Co Co.

Miss Wright asked Co Co if she played baseball.

Co Co murmured, "Non, Mademoiselle."

Miss Wright said, "You'll be okay." She slapped Co Co on the back and blew her whistle and Co Co jumped and stared at her. "OKAY, come on. Suzie and Ray will be captains today. Ray will have first choice. Come on, let's get going."

Co Co said, "Please, Mademoiselle, may I watch this game?"

Miss Wright nodded and Rich said, "I'll stay out and explain it to her."

The Select Seven pointed to Co Co and Rich and whispered and giggled until Miss Wright blew her whistle again and shouted, "Come on everybody, let's play ball."

When the teams were chosen and positions assigned, Ray, having given himself the favorite place as catcher, went up to bat. Professionally banging his bat on home plate, he yelled, "Batter up—batter up—come on—let's play ball!"

Suzie began the windup Rich and Ray had carefully taught her.

"Why does Suzie wave her arms?" Co Co whispered.

Rich said, "Every good pitcher does that, my girl, and Suzie is plenty good. You watch!"

Suzie pitched, there was a roar from the children, and Miss Wright called, "Strrr-i-k-e one!"

With a triumphant grin, Suzie caught the ball and wound up again. "Strrrr-i-k-e two!" "Strrr-i-k-e three! Ray's out!" The children roared and Suzie swaggered around in the middle of the field.

Rich said, "Come on, Co Co, old girl. You'll never play ball by watching."

The class yelled, "Come on, Co Co!"

Suzie ran over to her and whispered instructions. Co Co picked up the bat. Rich yelled, "Keep your eye on that ball, slugger." There was a loud whack and a roar of astonishment as Co Co's ball sailed over the heads of the fielders. "Run to first," Rich yelled. "Keep going to second—atta baby. Look at her go! Keep going!"

Suzie was jumping up and down, screaming, "It's a homer! Co Co, come on home—run!"

Like a streak of lightning, Co Co came in to home plate. Rich pounded her on the back. "Wow! What a slugger! Can you run! Oh baby!"

Co Co's eyes were gleaming as she said, "Oh baby! I like the base-*ball*!"

Miss Wright slapped her on the back. "French dressing is just what this team needs. Ha-ha!"

Rich muttered under his breath, "Oh that cornball and her jokes!" and Co Co giggled.

They played until Miss Wright blew her whistle.

"That's all for today. Don't dawdle."

The rest of the morning, in spite of admiring glances from the boys, and encouraging smiles from the girls, Co Co continued to sit with folded hands and downcast eyes.

Suzie whispered, "Miss Morrison wants school to be fun. She always tells us to relax and enjoy ourselves."

At lunch, Helen Blaine and Marjorie Desmond and Betsy Rhodes, and Linda and Penny and Barbara and even the Select Seven all fought to see who would sit next to Co Co and help her get her lunch and open her milk.

Co Co said, "Merci, merci!" to them all but sat next to Suzie and whispered, "They are kind, but I am not accustomed to children who shout."

After lunch the girls all trooped toward the benches under the willow tree to watch the boys play baseball. The Select Seven promptly surrounded Co Co and began to whisper and giggle. They completely ignored Suzie, whose eyes filled with tears, in spite of her determination to be brave and happy. She turned her back and thought, "Oh, if they get Co Co, too, I just don't know what I will do."

In a few moments Co Co came and sat down beside her. "Suzie, I do not know what they say. They speak fast and the numbers—it confuses me."

Millicent, always the spokesman for the Select Seven,

came over and stood in front of them. "Come on, Co Co. Gee whiz, it's an honor to be asked to join our club. We talk in code and call up boys and make them guess who is calling. Come on."

Co Co put her arm around Suzie. "And have you given my Suzie an invitation also?"

Millicent tossed her head. "Gosh no! Her mother's a teacher and she's a goody-goody and anyway she hasn't got a boyfriend."

Co Co gave her a chilly smile. "Merci. I think Suzie and I do not care for the club."

Millicent stuck her nose in the air. "OKAY, suit yourself. But you won't get asked again." She gathered up the Select Seven and they all stalked away.

Suzie said, "Oh thanks, Co Co, but you shouldn't have said no. They're all just neat girls—it's only the Select Seven—they don't mean to be snobby—it's Millicent."

Co Co shrugged. "You are my friend. If they do not have you, they do not have me. Now, tell me more about the school." The girls who were not in the Select Seven clustered around, and they all giggled and gossiped and had a dandy time.

They went to the Art Shack after lunch to choose the May Day posters. Suzie had been dreading this because two of the Select Seven were on the judging committee and she just *knew* hers wouldn't be chosen.

Miss Morrison suggested that Co Co be added to the committee, as a special courtesy. The posters were lined up against the wall, and the class marched solemnly by. Suzie heard Co Co say, "But Suzie is indeed an artist. It is excellent. It is a picture of the American school." She was even more astonished when she heard the rest of the committee eagerly agreeing with Co Co, and Suzie's poster was chosen to represent their class.

During social studies, Miss Morrison asked Co Co if she would mind pointing out on the map the various countries she had visited and telling something about each one. "It makes the countries seem so much more interesting to know someone who has been there," she added and smiled encouragingly.

Co Co blushed, but she walked up to the map and picked up the pointer. "If you will be so kind as to forgive my errors in English . . ." She had ridden on a camel and a donkey and an aerial tramway—she had traveled on canal boats and steamers and gondolas and trains and planes. She had skied in the Alps and had swum in the Mediterranean. The class all asked questions at once, and Co Co began to feel as if they were her friends instead of a group of strange children.

When the class was over, Suzie was so proud she said, right out loud, "Boy, Co Co, you make social studies seem just like television!"

Millicent turned around. "Well, teacher's pet, I

suppose you think you can talk out loud now, just because Co Co does!"

Suzie's eyes again filled with tears and she blushed. Whereupon Co Co leaned forward and said, "Taisez-vous Millicent! You are a beast!"

Millicent looked surprised but she said, "Tay zay voo? What does that mean? Can't you even speak English?"

Co Co raised one black eyebrow and said coldly, "Indeed I can. Taisez-vous means 'shut up.' Do not be rude to Suzie again."

Both Rich and Ray gave a howl of delighted laughter. "Atta girl, Co Co. Give it to her."

Fortunately the bell rang so Miss Morrison didn't have to say anything.

Chapter Five

A New Code

Every day Co Co came out from the hotel early in the morning and went to school with Suzie. She gradually lost her habit of sitting with downcast eyes and began to enjoy herself. She was formal and chilly to Millicent and the Select Seven, but friendly and natural with the other girls. Except for Rich and Ray, she was aloof with the boys until they complained to Suzie that she acted mad or something.

Friday morning on the way to school, Suzie said, "You don't have to act boy crazy, but you don't have to act as if boys were poison either. Johnny and Dick and Pete think you're mad at them."

Co Co's eyes glinted through her lashes. "I believe, Suzie, if I approved of the boy crazy, which I most certainly do not, I would smile at Rich. He is teaching me American words."

Suzie giggled. "If I approved of the boy crazy, which; I most certainly do not, I'd—I'd absolutely ignore them. Big smarties. Always showing off."

When they arrived at school, Miss Morrison said, "Let's settle down now and get as much done as possible before lunch. Then we can spend the afternoon working on the decorations. Remember, May Day is only one week away."

They all tried to settle down, but a warm spring wind blew through the open windows, flowering trees perfumed the air, birds sang as they flew back and forth. It was a lovely sunshiny day and everything outdoors seemed bent on distracting their attention from schoolwork.

Rich said, "Hey, Co Co, watch this!"

Miss Morrison turned from the board where she was explaining a long division problem, just in time to see Rich snap a rubber band and send a paper dart toward a fat robin perched on the window sill.

Miss Morrison sighed. "Rich, may I have your attention, please?"

Just then there was a knock at the door and a little girl from the second grade came in with a note. The children leaned forward to watch Miss Morrison read the note and then swiveled their necks around to watch the second grader. There was a burst of laughter when, as she opened the door to leave, a large shaggy gray dog walked solemnly up to Miss Morrison's desk and stood in front of the class.

Miss Morrison said, "Good morning, friend. Where did you come from?" and the class roared with laughter.

Ray said, "Oh, oh, he must have followed us."

Co Co left her desk and ran up to pat the dog as Millicent was saying, "Miss Morrison, that horrible old thing has been hanging around the school grounds all day. I think we should call the dogcatcher. He might have hydrophobia or something!"

There was a clamor of enraged protest from the children. Co Co came back to her desk and asked Suzie what a dogcatcher was.

"He is a man from the pound who drives around in a green truck and picks up dogs. The pound is kind of a dog hotel where stray animals are kept until their owners call for them."

"And if no one comes to get them?" Co Co asked.

Millicent turned around. "They gas them, and in case you don't understand plain English, that means they put them in a big tank and turn on the gas until they are dead."

Suzie roared, "Why Millicent Hansen! They do *not*! They put ads in the paper with pictures of the dogs, and people come and adopt them just like children."

The class all began to shout at once.

Miss Morrison said, "Children, children, calm down! Does anyone know where this dog lives?"

Ray made a hideous face at Millicent. "His name is Bravo and he lives on our block. His family have moved away, and he belongs to the whole neighborhood."

Bravo listened to this with great interest, yawned widely, and sat down and offered his paw to Miss Morrison. Miss Morrison shook his paw and told him he would probably enjoy chasing robins more than he would doing long division. She added, "Rich, you may be excused to take Bravo home."

Rich took hold of his collar, but Bravo obviously preferred school, for he braced his feet and slid, moaning and yelping, all the way to the door, much to the delight of the class.

They were just starting science when Rich came back and began a whispered report to Suzie and Co Co which the class all strained their ears to hear. Miss Morrison suggested that the twins help Co Co with her geological specimens while the rest of the class worked on the planets.

Rich and Ray and Co Co went over to the cabinet where the specimens were kept. Rich handed Co Co a rock. "This is feldspar. See the veins? Now what do you think this one is?"

Co Co shrugged and giggled. "Do you know what I think? I think they are all little stones and they resemble one another. I really do not care what the name is. Tell me more about what to say."

Rich picked up a couple of specimens of quartz and, keeping a weather eye on Miss Morrison, he resumed his coaching of all-important American playground speech. "Okay. Now when you're good and mad at a guy, you call him dumb, dopey, sappy, stinky, lousy, and knothead. Now you try it."

Instead of earnestly repeating the words after him, as she usually did, Co Co grinned wickedly. "I am bored with this louse-ey science, and this dumb dopey rock. I would prefer to speak of Bravo. Where is he?"

Ray gave a snort of laughter and said, "Jiggers— Miss Morrison!"

Rich picked up a piece of granite. "This is a vein of mica—we call it fool's gold."

Co Co leaned forward so her head was between theirs. "Tell me, do you and Ray prefer the Select Seven or do you prefer Suzie and me?"

Rich said, "Who wants to know?" and Ray added quickly, "We don't like girls—period. Now, pay attention to these rocks or we'll never get to the Art Shack."

After lunch, the weather was so lovely that Miss Morrison suggested that they collect their equipment and go out to the picnic tables under the big willow tree, instead of going to the Art Shack. She warned them to speak softly or they would disturb the rest of the school.

When they arrived at the willow tree, Bravo was lying on the grass panting. At the sight of the children he leapt to his feet and galloped over to Miss Morrison and offered her his paw. Miss Morrison sighed and said Bravo apparently preferred school. She told the boys to put their equipment on the table on the right side of the tree and the girls to sit at the table on the left side and finish cutting the streamers for the Maypoles.

For the next half hour it was fairly peaceful in the pale filtered sunshine under the willow tree. Then Millicent said, "Fourteen sure thinks she's smart because seventeen has a swimming pool. *We* think seventeen is stuck-up and snooty—even if she is half French. Half-baked is more like it."

The Select Seven giggled nervously and nudged each other.

Miss Morrison frowned. "Millicent, if you continue to be rude, I will have to take the class back into the room."

Millicent said, "I'm sorry, Miss Morrison," and made a face at Co Co.

Co Co leaned back and looked Millicent up and down. "Millicent, I believe I do not like that word ''alf baked.' Taisez-vous, s'il vous plaît, which, if you do not remember, means shut up, if you please."

Miss Morrison ignored this and said she had to go to the stock room for more supplies, and she expected the girls to govern themselves as if she were present.

The moment she was out of earshot, Millicent said, "Seventeen and fourteen wouldn't think they were so smart if they knew what four and five really thought about them. They think they're awful babies and goody-goodies and . . ."

Quick as a flash Suzie reached across the table and yanked Millicent's hair. "This baby's going to jerk all one's hair out by the roots if she doesn't shut up. If you say one more word in code I'll . . ." She looked up and saw Miss Morrison and blushed. "I'm awfully sorry, but she . . ."

"Just a moment, Suzie. I realize you have provocation, but you must not attack Millicent. Please apologize for pulling her hair."

Suzie muttered, "I'm sorry, Millicent." And under her breath added so Millicent could hear, "But you know darned well I'm not. I'll show you who's half-baked you old . . ."

Miss Morrison interrupted. "Perhaps now would be a good time to review the program. Dorothy, you're program chairman. Please read the schedule and then we'll discuss it."

Dorothy read and Suzie explained to Co Co the parts she didn't understand. Baseball games, songs, peasant dances, square dances and relay races. Just before the banquet, they would have the Maypole dances by all the classes together. The P.T.A. would provide the food. The banquet would be held in the lunchroom.

While the girls discussed their plans, Miss Morrison turned to the boys' table to see what they thought of the program.

During their discussion the girls all talked at once, Millicent's bossy voice louder than all the rest, until Co Co said, "I cannot hear and I do not understand. Suzie, your mother and my father can come to the banquet together, n'est-ce-pas?"

Millicent snorted, "Nes pa! Can't you ever speak English?" She turned to the Select Seven. "As long as fourteen's mother and seventeen's father are so darned crazy about each other, why don't they just give up and get married!"

Co Co jumped up and ran around the table, grabbed Millicent, and shook her. "Now, you have gone too far. You insult Suzie's mother and my papa. I will show you that I, too, know the American. You, Millicent, are dumb, dopey, sappy, stinkey, lousy, knothead. You are not grubby, but you are indeed ghastly and foul. Also you are the one unkind American child I have met. This time I, Clothilde Langdon, am going to punish you. This you will not forget!"

She stalked to the head of the table and stood in

Miss Morrison's place. Her eyes were blazing, her face was white, and she was shaking with rage. "Girls, may I have your attention please? Suzie, it is indeed loyal of you to quarrel with Millicent and the Sappy Seven to defend me." She swept them with a withering glance. "But me. I do not need defense. Now I will show you that I, too, can form the club. Will all the girls who are not of the Sappy Seven please join me after school under this willow tree?" She turned and stalked toward the Art Shack, her straight back eloquent of her intense disapproval.

When school was dismissed, Suzie and Sumiko and Marjorie and Betsy and Barbara and Linda and Penny clustered together under the tree, waiting for Co Co and saying, "Boy! She gets mad!" "Gosh, what a temper!" "Gee, I'm glad she's not mad at me!" "Gee, Suzie, what do you think she's going to do?"

Millicent and the Select Seven, gathered in another uneasy little group, wondered the same thing. Millicent tossed her head. "Well, I personally don't care what she does. I am *never* going to speak to Co Co again."

But her followers for once did not agree with her. Dorothy said, "Gee, Millicent, you really shouldn't have said that about her father," and the rest echoed, "Gosh no! You shouldn't ever be mean about parents." They wandered off casting worried looks at the group waiting for Co Co under the willow tree.

Suzie watched Co Co come running toward them, stop and speak to Miss Morrison, curtsy, and then come over to the bench. "Here you have the French Eight. Sit down, please, and attend." They sat down without speaking and waited for her to continue. "My friends, I have been thinking since I came to this American school. The Select Seven are ridiculous. Their code is not a secret code—it is the numbers of the seats of the children. All the world can understand it. Millicent is unkind to allow some of the children to be with her and to leave out others. She is rude. Me, I do not care to be rude—but I must punish Millicent. Eh, bien—now we, too, will have the secret code. We will speak French. When those poor idiots speak with the numbers, we will speak French, non?"

Sumiko asked Co Co timidly if it would not take a long time to learn to speak French.

Co Co answered, "Oh, we will not speak French, Sumiko. We will use French words to make them—oh, how do you say it?—we will make them irritable—furious—wild with anger. Me, I will speak French entirely. Even if you do not understand, which you probably will not, pretend that you do. That is what I do with English. I will write the French words and the way they sound, so you will appear to be speaking correctly." Co Co gave a triumphant shout of laughter. "Millicent will hate that!"

Suzie crowed, "Co Co, that's absolutely the neatest idea I've ever heard of in my life! Come on, everybody, let's go to my house and practice."

So, all the way home from school, Co Co walked backward and faced the French Eight. "Excuse me— 'excusez-moi.' Now you repeat it—'excusez-moi.'" Between bouts of hysterical giggles, the girls did their best to mimic Co Co. "Aykskeeusay mooah." They doubled up with laughter but they practiced.

Without a flicker of a smile, in Mademoiselle's most stern manner, Co Co drove them on. "Again—again. It is not good, but it will have to do. Now—what do you want?—'Que voulez-vous?'" Again they tried and again they laughed so hard they could barely speak. "Kuh voolayvoo—oh, it sounds so funny!" Co Co shook her head. "Do not laugh. Again—again—'que voulez-vous.'"

Barbara said, "But it sounds awful when we try it."

Co Co shrugged, "It is not perfect, but Millicent will not know. She is an idiot. Again—'que voulez-vous.'"

They chanted "kuh voolayvoo" over and over again until Co Co said, "Good—good! Now—come here— 'venez ici.'"

Before they had reached Mrs. Medlin's gate, they were saying "vaynay seesee" so even Co Co was pleased. They stopped short when they heard Mrs.

Medlin shouting, "Get *out*! Don't ever step one foot in this yard again! Don't let me see your faces even looking over this hedge!" They watched two small boys backing slowly up the walk with Mrs. Medlin shaking her finger right under their noses. She shoved them through the gate with a final, "Now *scat*!" The boys ran down the street shouting, "Old Medler Medlin! Old Medler Medlin!"

Co Co said, "'Je n'aime pas cette mèchante sorcière.' It means—I do not like that wicked witch!"

She had no trouble at all teaching her eager pupils, "Zhuh naym pah set meshant soorsair!"

Grandmother gave them all cookies and lemonade, and they settled down around the kitchen table to practice. By five o'clock they were still getting mixed up and saying, "What did you say?" when they meant, "Come here," but they sounded French enough to annoy Millicent, and Co Co and Suzie promised to spend the weekend writing eight copies of the French code.

Chapter Six

The Boys
Have a Code Also

Co Co stayed all night with Suzie, and Saturday morning they got up very early and made eight copies of the French code. Suzie was all for having just as many phrases as Millicent had numbers, but Co Co was firm. "No, Suzie, no. We wish to annoy the Select Seven—not to teach them."

After breakfast they went to Co Co's house to see what the workmen had accomplished during the week. Paint cans and ladders and canvas littered every room, but the woodwork already had a coat of white paint and the Pink House was beginning to look cheerful and more as Suzie had always imagined it. Co Co's room was to be papered in blue, and the guest room, which Co Co called Suzie's room, was to be exactly like it in pink. The bathroom between the two rooms was so torn up they couldn't get into it, but Co Co said, "Papa and I found the picture in a magazine. It is beautiful like the cinema—not at all like a French bathroom."

The kitchen also was all torn up, and Mrs. MacGregor was scurrying around emptying boxes and lining drawers and grumbling that modern kitchens were all very well, but at the rate the workmen were going, hers wouldn't be ready by Christmas.

Both Co Co and Suzie were a little afraid of Mrs. MacGregor, although Grandmother said her bark was worse than her bite. But when she called them for lunch and produced chicken sandwiches and hot chocolate and fresh cupcakes, they decided she was probably like Grandmother—prickly on the outside, but warm and friendly on the inside.

That afternoon, while Suzie's mother went shopping with Co Co's father to pick out wallpaper and furniture, Suzie and Co Co decided to stay home and play in the Lookout. They spent the whole afternoon looking through magazines and choosing glamorous furniture for their bedrooms.

Suzie's mother asked Co Co to stay for dinner, but Mr. Langdon said they were going to have a farewell dinner for Mademoiselle as she was leaving for France on Sunday afternoon. So Grandmother suggested that they come back from taking Mademoiselle to the plane and have Sunday night supper instead.

Sunday evening, when they arrived for supper, Co Co's eyes were red from crying and Mr. Langdon seemed quite sad, too. He said, "Mademoiselle disliked America very much, and she could hardly wait to get back to France, but she has been with us so long, it was almost like saying good-bye to a member of the family."

Co Co's eyes filled with tears. "I did not realize. I thought I would be glad because Mademoiselle would not scold anymore. But when she walked up the steps of the plane and waved to me, I cried and cried. She is almost like my mother. I will miss her so much." Co Co burst out crying again.

Suzie's mother cuddled her and Grandmother said, "I have an idea. Suppose you plan to stay here with us until your house is finished. We have plenty of room, and it's perfect nonsense for you to have to take a taxi out from the hotel every morning. Then you can get used to your new relatives."

Mr. Langdon thanked her but said he would have to stay at the hotel. He had so many conferences it would really be easier for them to stay right where they were. But Suzie and Co Co begged so hard and promised to be so good and helpful that he finally consented to let Co Co stay, at least until her room was finished.

The idea of living at Grandmother's house cheered Co Co up so much that she ate three servings of everything and chattered about how awful Millicent was, just as if she'd always lived with Suzie.

After supper they drove down to the hotel and got Co Co's luggage and spent a joyful evening, dividing up bureau drawers and closet space. Suzie even gave Co Co half of her signed movie star pictures to hang over her bed. Then they went to bed and giggled and planned what they were going to do to the Select Seven on Monday.

Suzie said, "I know, we'll get up early tomorrow and call up everybody in the French Eight and tell them to meet us under the willow tree at eight o'clock."

Co Co bounced in her bed and laughed. "Those Sappy Seven. They will be furious!"

So, on Monday morning, Miss Morrison was just as astonished as the Select Seven, when she was greeted by eight "bonjour, Mademoiselle Morrison"s, followed by hysterical giggles. All morning long "Pardonnezmoi" peppered the classroom, and there were many unnecessary and self-conscious references to the day being "lundi."

Co Co seemed to have thrown away her English entirely. She spoke only French, even when Miss Morrison suggested that she repeat her answers in English. Even Sumiko, although sitting right under the clock, kept asking Miss Morrison, "Quelle heure est-il?" She asked the time, however, in such a soft voice that only Millicent heard her, and she kept saying, "For gosh sakes, I suppose you think it's smart to ask what time it is in French."

Miss Morrison's face was twitching with laughter, but she behaved just as if this sudden French invasion were perfectly normal and even answered Co Co in French. Millicent's hand was waving all morning just like a signal flag as she tattled on first one and then another of the French Eight.

At recess Ray said, "Hey, you guys. I've got an idea." The boys clustered around him and began a whispered consultation. After that all sixteen boys began to talk pig Latin. Rich and Ray held out the sides of their trousers and flounced up to the eight French code speakers. They curtsied elaborately and said in unison, "Irls-gay are-yay or-may umb-day an-thay usual oo-tay ay-day, ont-day ou-yay ink-thay o-say?"

Rich trilled in a high squeaky voice, "Efinitely-day, my dear Alphonse."

Ray answered, "Efinitely-day, my dear Gaston," and they held their hands in front of their mouths and giggled just the way the Select Seven did.

Suzie looked haughty. "Oh stop it, Ray. You make me sick!"

Ray jerked her arm. "Who's making who sick, that's what I'd like to know? Now listen, Suzie, you and Co Co are pretty good ball players, but you're not so sharp that you can fool around acting like a couple of sissies. Now cut it out."

Rich said, "Co Co, for gosh sakes, wise up. Cut out all this French nonsense and stuff and come on and play ball."

Co Co said primly, "Monsieur Rich, French is not what you call nonsense nor is it stuff. It is the language of love!"

The French Eight giggled and twined their arms around one another. Co Co switched up to Rich and Ray. "You say you do not like the girls. Then, you go with the boys." Co Co led her group off giggling and whispering.

After lunch the classroom was in complete confusion. The boys giggled and talked pig Latin, the French Eight repeated their phrases even when they weren't called on, and the Select Seven tattled without raising their hands.

When it was time for social studies they were being so silly and making so much noise, Miss Morrison rapped on her desk with her ruler. Her face wore the stern expression she used only when there were serious breaks of the school rules. "Boys, you are to be quiet immediately. Millicent and Suzie, please bring me your codes."

Millicent made a face at Co Co as she rummaged in her desk. With an injured expression and a muttered,

"Teacher's pets, this is all your fault," she tossed her long list of numbers on Miss Morrison's desk. Suzie trembled as she handed Miss Morrison her carefully copied French phrase list.

Miss Morrison didn't even smile as she said, "I thought this class was far enough advanced to have the schedule changed and interrupted. Obviously I was mistaken. I am particularly disappointed because next year I am going to teach French in junior high school. I was looking forward to having some of you in that class. Today, I do not feel that I wish to teach you anything next year."

There was a long-drawn-out flurry of, "I'm sorry, Miss Morrison," followed by a dead silence.

Still without smiling, Miss Morrison continued, "Learning French phrases is an excellent idea, but I cannot approve of any code or group of words that is used to exclude other members of the class." She glanced meaningly at Millicent, who flounced around in her seat, but the rest of the Select Seven hung their heads and looked guilty.

Co Co raised her hand. "Mademoiselle Morrison—this rude behavior—I thought the Sept Choisies, the Select Seven, were unkind to Suzie. I punished them with the French code." Her mouth quivered and her eyes filled with tears. "I am sorry—and if you will please pardon me—I will not be rude again."

Miss Morrison smiled at last. "Very well, Co Co. I think we all understand one another now. Co Co, last week, you said you had spent one summer at Languedoc and Carcassonne. Suppose you point out the area on the map and tell us what you remember of that feudal city. You may use French phrases whenever you care to, and we will see how much we can understand."

The class had never been as quiet and attentive as it was while Co Co described the great walled towers of Carcassonne. She spattered French words right and left, and obligingly translated as she told of the moats and the city within the walls, just like the pictures of witch's castles in fairy tale books. Her face glowed with pride as she finished, "and on Bastille Day—it is a day of liberty, like the American Fourth of July—they shoot fireworks in front of the battlements—the towers are golden and sparkling in the light of the rockets. I wish I could show you Carcassonne on Bastille Day. It is so beautiful."

Rich raised his hand. "Gosh, Miss Morrison. If you listen carefully, you can almost tell what the French words mean. I sure wish you would give us a chance at that French class."

Ray added quickly, "I'll bet Co Co would help us and then I'll bet you'd sure be proud of us in French."

Miss Morrison said, "Well, we'll see," and smiled.

When Co Co saw that Miss Morrison looked less

Mary Bard

angry, she said, "Miss Morrison, I have an invitation for the class from Papa. Our house is not completed as yet, but Papa would like you to come to a picnic—a French and American picnic. It is to celebrate our first house and our first neighborhood and my first American school. Papa thought we should have it the day we have dress rehearsal for May Day. We will have French dishes and also the hamburger and the hot dog." She grinned at Miss Morrison and sat down.

The class clapped and all began to talk about the picnic, the bell rang, and Miss Morrison sighed with relief.

Chapter Seven

The French and American Picnic

The day of the picnic, Co Co was so worried for fear everything wouldn't be ready and the class would not enjoy themselves, she could hardly eat breakfast. She had decided to surprise Suzie and not let her see the bedrooms until they were all finished. She had gotten up early and gone down to the Pink House to see that everything in her room was in its place, but at breakfast she fussed and fumed. "Suzie, we should not have invited them to the housewarming. The house is not warm—it is cold—it is a field of battle! Paint cans—ladders! And Madame MacGregor is a thundercloud."

"Oh, don't worry. I can hardly wait to see Millicent's face when she sees the swimming pool. And the Select Seven!"

Grandmother added, "It's a beautiful day and there

isn't one thing for you to worry about."

Co Co said, "Thank you, Grand'mère. I will try not to worry."

When they got to school there was so much excitement, Co Co didn't have a chance to worry about the picnic. Miss Morrison handed each child a long list of duties and said they'd have to work fast. She asked Co Co to help Suzie. The class, with years of May Day experience behind them, rushed in and out of the room, organizing the other classes and checking last-minute details. Suzie handed Co Co a bunch of May Day programs and told her to clip them together after she'd sorted them out, then tore out of the room to check the kindergarten.

Every time Suzie came back to her desk, Co Co handed her a note. "Do you think Madame MacGregor will know how to cook chicken?"—"Do you think Papa will remember to get the cake at the pastry shop?"

Suzie always answered, "Relax, relax. Oh my gosh, the second-grade sunbonnets . . ." and dashed out of the room again.

Right after lunch the whole school marched out on the playground. The schoolyard rang with last-minute instructions from the harried teachers, calls for the square dances, and music from the record player. Hammers banged, saws buzzed, bells rang, and over it all sounded the bossy voices of the sixth grade as they dashed from group to group, supervising the costumes and decorations.

Co Co was upset by the strangeness and confusion. She followed Miss Morrison around saying, "I do not know what to do," until Miss Morrison patted her comfortingly and said, "Don't worry, Co Co. Tomorrow the whole thing will unwind as smoothly as a ribbon. You go and help Suzie."

But finding Suzie proved to be quite a difficult feat. Co Co caught an occasional glimpse of her running toward the lunchroom, weaving in and out of the shouting children, or staggering under a load of costumes.

Finally Co Co just sat down on the school steps and gave up. She felt just as strange and alone as if she'd arrived in America that day. She watched all the shouting children and murmured, "Mademoiselle was right when she told Papa that I would not understand the American school."

She was beginning to feel thoroughly sorry for herself, when Suzie appeared in front of her. "Where on earth have you been, Co Co? I've been hunting and hunting for you. You'll have to watch these kindergartners for me. Everybody else is too busy. Think of something to amuse them, and for heaven's sake, don't let one of them out of your sight!"

She took Co Co over to a group of equally bewildered little children and darted off again.

Co Co dropped down in the middle of the ring of tired children and began a spirited song, "Le Bon Roi Dagobert." At the strange sound of the French words, the children all squatted down around her, sat perfectly still, and watched her with fascinated eyes. No longer did she feel strange and useless, for the kindergartners stuck to her like paste and demanded more and more songs.

When the final dress rehearsal was announced over the loud speaker, Suzie appeared again and gathered up the small children and shepherded them away. The noise and shouting stopped, order was restored and, much to Co Co's astonishment, the program unwound just like a satin ribbon.

After it was over, Mr. Wagner mopped his forehead and announced that everything was ready for the best possible May Day, and school was dismissed.

There was much excitement over the prospect of the picnic as Suzie's mother and Miss Morrison led the way to Co Co's house. They were followed by a line of giggling, boisterous children.

Suzie drew a long, ecstatic breath of delight when they finally wound down the driveway and came around the Pink House, which glowed in the late afternoon sunlight. Bright flowers bloomed in all the planting boxes in the patio, music came from the record player, and all around the pool were colored lawn chairs.

Under the trees was stretched a long picnic table with baskets of flowers and a present in front of each place. It was more glamorous than any movie party Suzie had ever imagined!

From the barbecue pit, Mr. Langdon called out, "Welcome—welcome to the sixth grade!" Then he walked around and shook hands with everybody.

Grandfather seated Suzie's mother and Miss Morrison in lawn chairs, handed them tall glasses of iced tea, and told them to relax and enjoy themselves—everything was under control.

Grandmother said they were going to have an early supper so to hurry up and change their clothes and by the time they were through swimming, supper would be ready.

Mr. Langdon showed the boys to the dressing room under the patio, and Co Co took the girls to her room. Suzie gasped when she opened the door. It was just like a movie bedroom! Pale-blue-and-white-striped walls, pale-blue curtains and bedspreads, a thick white rug on the floor, but best of all—studio couches with bookcases of blond mahogany, modern chests of drawers, and a dressing table with a big square mirror. "Oh, Co Co, it's just perfect! It's just like a college girl's room. I can't believe it!"

Co Co said, "But wait, there is more." She opened the door of the bathroom. Pale-blue fixtures, blue tiled walls, and pink-and-blue-striped wallpaper. She turned to Suzie. "But now, your room. I hope you like it."

Co Co opened the door of the guest room and Suzie couldn't even speak she was so excited. It was pale pink, but other than the color, it was exactly like Co Co's room, even to the dressing table with the big square mirror. The French Eight and even the Select Seven were equally thrilled and excited. All the time they were getting into their bathing suits, they kept up a steady stream of admiration for Co Co's beautiful house and garden.

Co Co was just as pleased and excited as everyone else until Millicent tossed her head and said, "Well, your room *is* pretty, but personally I never did like blue or pink. My room is yellow and I have frilly curtains and a ruffled bedspread. My Aunt Mabel says the weather is much too cold for swimming and anyway, she won't allow me to swim in public pools." She opened her beach bag and took out a frilly pink sundress. "I have thousands of sundresses, but I brought this old one because pink is four's favorite color."

The girls were so shocked at Millicent's rude behavior that they kept perfectly still as she sat down in front of the mirror and preened and patted herself. Suzie recovered first and marched over to her. "Millicent Hansen, you make me sick! You're just jealous and you know it. Personally, I'm glad you're not going swimming. You'd probably pollute the water."

The Select Seven did not gather around Millicent and stick up for her. Instead, they gathered around Co Co and said they thought her room was beautiful, and they could hardly wait to swim in her pool and Millicent was mean and she'd be sorry she didn't bring her bathing suit.

Millicent didn't pay the least bit of attention. She continued to wind her curls around her finger and admire herself in the mirror. "My aunt Mabel says boys don't like foreigners and rough girls, and personally, I don't either." She gave Co Co a haughty glance and sauntered out of the room.

Suzie put her hands on her hips. "Well, of all the conceited, jealous, rude . . . !"

Dorothy, who was second in command of the Select Seven, walked over and put her arm around Co Co. "Don't you pay one bit of attention to Millicent. She's just dying to go swimming. She told me so, but her aunt Mabel won't let her, because she might spoil her permanent. We won't even speak to that old Millicent!"

The rest of the Select Seven echoed, "We certainly won't. We won't even speak to Millicent."

Ten minutes later, the garden pool was a seething mass of splashing, shouting boys and girls. Mr. Langdon, who was building a fire in the outdoor fireplace, called out that the pool was twelve feet deep at the end where the bridge was, and it was perfectly safe to dive. Johnny Allen promptly climbed up on the bridge and did a swan dive. Suzie, who had waited for years to swim in the garden pool, did an expert flip and almost landed on Sumiko. Ray dove in and came up beside Suzie. "That's a neat dive, Suze, old girl. Let's have a race to see who can swim across the pool and back the fastest."

Rich called out, "Hey, Sumiko, you and Johnny and Dorothy go first. Ready—get set—dive!"

In one swift movement, Sumiko dove like a seal, swam under water halfway down the pool, rose to a perfectly timed crawl, turned, and swam back so powerfully that she won by a length of the pool. There were cries of astonishment. "Boy! Did you see that?" "Boy, can she swim!" and "Where did you learn to swim like that?"

Sumiko smiled shyly as she shook the water from her ears. "In Japan. My brother is on the swimming team. He taught us to swim when we were little." Sumiko was surrounded by admiring boys who asked her to teach them.

Millicent stood watching this. Then she climbed up on the bridge and carefully arranged her skirt, crossed her legs, and pointed her toes. She called, "Did any of you boys bring a camera?" She took a mirror out of her pocket and began to put on lipstick.

"*Millicent*, what'll Miss Morrison say?" The girls

were torn between admiration for her daring and disapproval of the lipstick.

Suzie watched the sunlight glisten through Millicent's curls, the pink sundress reflected on her cheeks. Millicent also wore pink fingernail polish and pink toenail polish. Suzie sighed enviously and said to Co Co, "Gosh, no wonder the boys have secrets with her. Just look at her. She's practically as pretty and grown up as a movie star."

Co Co set her lips and said primly, "I am glad Mademoiselle is not here. What she would say to see a young girl wearing lipstick! And pink fingernails and toenails. I'm sorry, but I do not approve of Millicent's behavior at all."

Rich and Ray suddenly appeared on the bridge behind Millicent. They winked at Suzie and Co Co, said, "Unk-day?"—"Ight-ray" and quick as a flash, dumped Millicent in the pool.

She came up gasping and shrieking. "Gosh, now look what you've done! You've ruined my brand-new pink sundress. And *my permanent*! Aunt Mabel will just about kill me!"

Rich said casually, "Sorry about the dress, old girl."

Ray grinned. "How else do you wash off lipstick?" he asked, and the whole class doubled up with laughter.

Millicent tossed her head. "Now that I'm all wet, I might as well swim." With that, she climbed up on the bridge, did a double jackknife, and swam across the pool almost as fast as Sumiko.

Suzie's heart dropped as Rich said, "Gosh! Who'd ever think old Mil could swim?"

Ray called, "Hey, Mil, I'll race you."

Millicent was silly and coy. She simpered and had to be begged, but she beat everyone but Sumiko, and then did back flips and swan dives until the whole class was standing around and admiring her.

Suzie was so disgusted she turned her back, just as Bravo's large furry gray head forced its way through Mrs. Medlin's hedge, breaking several branches off in the process. He gave one yelp of joy, ran over, and jumped in the pool.

Millicent began to shriek. "Get me out of here! Help, help!"

Hearing her cry for help, Bravo swam toward her, grabbed the ruffle on the back of her sundress, and tugged and pulled and jerked her down to the shallow end of the pool. Millicent struggled out, yelling, "Filthy, dirty old dog!" and rushed into the house.

But the rest of the class took turns jumping, crying, "Help" and being rescued until they were all completely exhausted.

Mr. Langdon called out that supper was almost ready and they'd better hurry up and get dressed.

While the girls were dressing, Suzie said, "Heavens

to Betsy! I almost forgot! We're supposed to give Miss Morrison her shower, right after supper!"

Co Co stuck a horrified face out of her petticoat. "Suzie, what do you say? You are not going to bathe Miss Morrison!"

The girls looked mystified for a minute and then burst out laughing. Even Suzie's face was red with suppressed laughter as she tried to explain a shower to Co Co. "We aren't really going to give Miss Morrison a shower. I mean, a shower isn't a bath. It's a shower—I mean . . ." Suzie tried all over again, but the more she tried to explain, the more horrified Co Co looked.

Even Millicent was giggling so hard she could barely speak. "Co Co, it's like the bark of a dog and the bark on a tree. The words are the same but they don't mean the same thing. A shower is a bath—but it's also a party you give for somebody who is going to get married."

Co Co threw up her hands. "The shower is not the shower—it is the shower! Come, let us have supper. That I understand."

Just as they were starting out the door, Millicent held out her hand to Co Co. "I'm sorry I've been so mean, Co Co. I'd just give anything to have a house like this with a pool and everything."

Suzie heaved a sigh of relief and they all went downstairs and ran out into the garden.

There were shouts of "Wow!" and "Boy!" and "Good

for Co Co!" as they sat down at the long table. There were platters of potato salad, green salad, and fruit salad. There was French chicken mousse and jellied parslied ham and American hamburgers and hot dogs.

Everybody was so hungry that no matter how many hamburgers and hot dogs Grandfather brought to the table, they were gone in a flash and the children were shouting for more. They thought the French chicken and ham were delicious. After they'd eaten so much they could barely swallow, Co Co excused herself and came back carrying a French birthday cake with thirteen birthday candles sitting in tiny cream puffs around the edge. She placed the cake in front of Sumiko. "Happy birthday! It is French ice cream spongecake and it is my favorite."

They all sang, "Happy Birthday" to Sumiko and Mr. Langdon said, "We are indeed honored to have you with us on your birthday, Sumiko."

Sumiko's lovely little face was golden with joy as she gazed at the flickering candles. The children shouted, "Make a wish—make a wish!" and Sumiko said softly, "I wish Co Co and I may always live happily in America."

Mr. Langdon said, "Now, if you will each open the package in front of your places, you will receive a present from Co Co because you have all been so kind to her."

They opened their gifts and found that each one had a ballpoint pen with his or her name on it.

Meanwhile the girls had been whispering excitedly to one another. Suzie and Co Co asked to be excused and went into the house. They came back carrying a large package which they placed in front of Miss Morrison. Co Co said, "Dear Mademoiselle Morrison—this bath—pardon—shower—is for you from the class with best wishes." She giggled helplessly when Miss Morrison opened a set of bath towels embroidered with a large "W." "Pardon, please pardon, but the present. It is also for the shower." She leaned against Suzie and laughed until the tears ran down her face, as she told her father about the two kinds of showers.

Meanwhile, Bravo, who had been happily swimming in the pool all through dinner and catching bits of hot dog and hamburger, decided he must be missing something. He came out of the pool, walked up to Mr. Langdon, and shook himself.

Mr. Langdon laughed. "This is still another kind of a shower, Co Co. Who owns this sopping wet, but delightfully friendly dog?"

Rich said that he belonged to their whole block, but nobody really owned him.

Co Co said, "Papa, could we own Bravo so he would not have to go to the Pound Hotel?"

Mr. Langdon shook his head. "Well, I'd planned to

get a hunting dog and Bravo isn't exactly my idea of a hunter, but I'll think it over." He turned to the children. "Co Co and I wish to thank you for a delightful housewarming. We hope you will come and swim and play tennis as often as you like. Miss Morrison says you have a very important day ahead of you tomorrow, and I promised her I wouldn't keep you up late. So if you will gather up your bathing suits, we will drive you home."

Rich and Ray walked over to him. "We think you should know that Bravo belongs on our block. We all take care of him. He doesn't need another home. Thank you very much for the party. We had a nice time." They each took hold of one of Bravo's ears, and marched out of the garden.

Johnny Allen asked Suzie, "How come they're so huffy all of a sudden?" But Suzie didn't pay any attention in the flurry of good-byes.

When they had all left, Suzie and Co Co helped carry the things into the kitchen, thanked Mrs. MacGregor for all her trouble, and told her it was the best food they'd ever tasted. Then Suzie said, "I know—let's lie in the garden chairs and pretend we're movie stars and have on beautiful fluffy party dresses and we've just come home from a great big dance."

Co Co sighed and sat down in a garden chair and stared out over the pool.

Suzie asked, "What's the matter? Didn't you like the picnic?" She saw two large tears on Co Co's cheeks.

Co Co sniffed. "Yes, it was delightful, but Rich is angry with me." She turned her head away.

Suzie said, "Oh, he'll get over it. He always does." But she was much more worried than she sounded. Co Co was the first best friend she had ever had and she dreaded to ask the question she knew she must ask, even if it meant that she would lose her friend.

Suzie felt just as if she were holding her nose and jumping off the fifty-foot board as she said, "Co Co, you're not turning boy crazy are you?"

Co Co sobbed, "I—don't—know. Rich is the first American boy—who was kind to me and now—I know in my heart—he does not like me—anymore." She buried her head in her arms and cried harder than ever.

Suzie felt lonelier than she had ever felt in her life as she patted Co Co's shoulder. "Oh, I'm sure he likes you, Co Co. I'm sure he likes you best."

Chapter Eight

May Day

May Day morning when Suzie looked out the window to see if Co Co was up, she found the mountains invisible and the garden shrouded in a thin white mist. "Oh darn! Everything happens to me lately!" She pulled the covers up over her head. "First, Co Co will get boy crazy, then she'll put her hair up in pin curls and wear lipstick, then she'll join the Select Seven and act snippy and have secrets. I just can't stand it if Co Co begins to act that way."

Jet whined and scratched at the door to tell her breakfast was ready. Suzie shuffled over to let him in. "A lot you care whether it rains. You always wear the same outfit. I'll bet Co Co won't even remember to wear her new dress, she's so busy thinking about Rich and being boy crazy. Boys make me sick—period!"

Suzie jerked on her clothes, pulled her new plaid dress over her head, and sat down in front of the mirror. The face that looked back at Suzie was all crumpled with sleepiness. Her mouth turned down at the corners, her eyes were little blue slits, and her bangs were every which way like spilled toothpicks.

She yanked the brush through her hair. "I don't care if everybody in the world except me turns boy crazy. I just hate boys!"

She shuffled down the stairs and into the kitchen, grumbled, "Morning," to her grandmother, and glared out the window toward Co Co's house.

Grandmother said, "It seems kind of lonely, now that Co Co's moved home, doesn't it? What's the matter? Did you get up out of the wrong side of the bed?"

"You can't expect me to say good morning, when it's obviously just about the worst morning anybody ever saw."

Grandmother shook her head. "Tsk-tsk! 'Red sky at night, sailor's delight.' Yesterday was beautiful with a bright red sunset and today will be just as nice."

Suzie sat down at the table. "Just my luck. Every single year it's been sunshiny, and now, just because *we're* graduating, it'll probably pour buckets." Suzie's mouth was full of French toast, but Grandmother could still make out "darned old rain! Sopping wet Maypoles—everything happens to me!"

Grandmother began her count-your-blessings lecture, but Suzie went right on muttering.

Just then Co Co pushed open the back door. "Bonjour, Grand'mère, Hi, Suzie! Even the mist is keeping the May Day a surprise. You wear your new dress—I wear mine also." Her eyes shone and her hair twinkled with mist droplets. She pulled out a chair and sat down.

She talked on about sleeping in her new bed and taking a bath in her new bathroom and how Suzie must hurry and sleep in her new room to see if it was as comfortable as Suzie's room at home. She didn't seem to notice Suzie's gloomy silence.

Meanwhile Suzie was looking her over very carefully for the obvious signs of boy craziness. Co Co's hair was still straight and shining, she didn't seem to be sad, and although she had already eaten one breakfast, she was busily eating French toast. She certainly wasn't one bit like Millicent.

Co Co went right on talking while she took a second piece of French toast and put three large spoonfuls of wild blackberry jam on it. "Ummmmm, this is delicious. Now, if I were in Paris, I would know that the sun is hiding his head and would wake up at noon and come smiling out. But in Seattle . . ." She shrugged.

Grandmother laughed. "Rain or shine, Co Co, I

never saw a child relish food the way you do. I declare, you must have a hollow leg."

Co Co stuck her legs out and looked at them. "Hollow? That means empty, does it not? No, Grand'mère, they are the same as the legs of Suzie."

At last Suzie giggled. Rain or shine, boy crazy or not, Co Co was the neatest, most fun, best friend anybody ever had.

They finished their breakfast and Grandmother kissed them both. "Now, on your way to school, look over Mrs. Medlin's hedge. That woman is a regular barometer. If she's working in her garden, I absolutely guarantee it won't rain."

They stopped and peeped over the hedge and there was Mrs. Medlin, wearing a floppy garden hat, dark glasses, and a sleeveless sweater.

Co Co grabbed Suzie's arm. "Look, Bravo is in the rhododendron!"

Sure enough, Bravo was winding in and out of the flower beds, sniffing the blossoms as he passed. "I hope she doesn't turn around." Suzie gasped. "She'll have a fit and call the dogcatcher."

"Quick Suzie, whistle to him. He will hate it in the Pound Hotel."

Suzie gave a short low whistle, and Bravo cocked his ears, saw the girls, and barked. Then he ran over and leapt on Mrs. Medlin, knocked her over, and licked her face. She roared, "*Get out!* Get out, you gray horror. I don't see how you get in the yard all the time. I'm going right into the house and calling the pound."

Suzie whistled again, and Bravo came bounding toward them, scattering rhododendron blossoms like snowflakes in his wake. Mrs. Medlin grabbed a rake and started after him.

Suzie called, "Come here, Bravo, quickly. You'll have to go to school with us. Hurry—run!"

As they all tore down the street, they could hear Mrs. Medlin shouting, "It won't do you girls one bit of good to take that dog to school with you. I'll tell the dogcatcher where he is."

Co Co called over her shoulder. "Old witch! You will not catch Bravo. We will hide him. Old witch!"

When they got to school Suzie was worried. "I hope she doesn't call the principal. If she makes enough fuss, Mr. Wagner will have to call the pound."

Co Co stamped her foot. "Name of a name! I will tell Mr. Wagner that he would not dare!" Co Co was showing all the signs of working herself up, her eyes were blazing, her face was white, and she was breathing fast.

Co Co began to mutter in French, and Suzie was greatly relieved to hear the bell ring. Co Co stamped into the line. "I will also stamp on the rhododendron of Mrs. Medlin. I will pick the flowers and throw them on the ground. If she chases me, I will throw her some dirt. I will . . ."

Rich turned around. "Wow, you sound dangerous this morning! What's the matter?"

Co Co waved her arms, spoke half French and half English, and stamped her foot. She certainly wasn't acting one bit like Millicent, and she certainly didn't seem to be boy crazy.

Rich said, "Take it easy, chum. Relax. It won't be the first time somebody has called the dogcatcher for old Bravo. He's been to the pound a couple of times. But he's plenty smart. The minute he sees that old green truck, he just fades."

When they got into the classroom, Miss Morrison handed out the May Day duty slips. Suzie and Co Co opened the door to go down to the kindergarten room, and Bravo sneaked in, grinning foolishly.

Miss Morrison said they did not need Bravo's assistance on May Day of all days and asked Rich and Ray to take him home and lock him up.

Rich and Ray promised to put Bravo in their furnace room. They took hold of his ears and again he slid, moaning, to the door.

The class spent the rest of the morning, checking costumes for the various groups and clipping programs together. Millicent was so busy bossing the seating arrangements for the banquet that she didn't have much time to whisper, but did say to Dorothy, "Guess what? Ten called eight and his mother said she'd tell the telephone company if she called anymore and ten said . . ."

Co Co leaned forward and seemed to be listening to Millicent with great interest. Suzie's heart dropped again.

What if she is just memorizing the number code? Suzie thought. What if she decides to become a Select Seven?

She was quiet for such a long time that Co Co finally noticed her silence. "Suzie, do not disturb yourself. I think Seattle is like Paris and the sun is hiding in the clouds." Suzie said, huffily, "I'm not worrying about the sun."

"You are quiet today. What is it that disturbs you?"

Suzie sighed. "Promise you won't get mad if I tell you?" Co Co nodded and Suzie put her hand in front of her mouth so Millicent couldn't hear. "You remember last night—when you said Rich didn't like you anymore? I asked you then but you didn't answer. Well, do you think you are turning boy crazy?"

Co Co didn't answer for a minute. A little smile played around her mouth, and she looked through her lashes at Suzie. "I do not behave like Millicent, but yes, I like Rich the best."

Suzie slumped in her seat. "Honestly! I just don't

think I can stand it if you talk in code and wear pin curls."

"No, Suzie, no! This is what I believe. You are not pleased when Ray appears to prefer Millicent. I also am not pleased when she calls Rich on the telephone. I would like to scratch her. Yes, I like Rich the best and I think if you will look in your heart, you like Ray the best also."

Suzie heaved a large sigh of relief, and they finished clipping their programs in silence.

The May Day program began at two o'clock. Just as the children marched out onto the playground, the sun burst through the clouds and shone on the schoolyard, spotlighting the cheerful costumes. The trees sparkled with raindrops, the mothers smiled with anticipation, the Maypoles stood proudly, their ribbons blowing in the soft May wind, and the rings of children looked like wreaths of brilliant flowers.

"Now the school appears like your beautiful picture! You are indeed an artist, Suzie." Co Co danced along beside Suzie at the head of the kindergartners.

Miss Daly played "London Bridge" on the piano, but the little children stood perfectly still and begged Co Co to sing for them. Then two of them spied their mothers and started toward the audience. Suzie ran after them and Co Co tried to put her arms around the rest. "Quick, Suzie, I cannot hold them all. Aren't they adorable in their stiff little frocks and pantaloons? They make me think of a flock of butterflies."

"More like an anthill right after you've poked it. Oh, what are we going to do?" Suzie grabbed wildly in all directions.

Miss Daly left the piano and said calmly, "Let us play Clap, Clap, Curtsy, the game we play before we go home—remember?"

At this familiar suggestion, the children began enthusiastic off-key singing, stamping and bowing, and then clapped much more loudly than their mothers when they were through.

Co Co was delighted but Suzie mopped her brow. "Wow! I'm glad that's over." They distributed the little children to their mothers and settled down to enjoy themselves.

The first and second grades did folk dances, and Co Co clapped and shouted, "Bravo! Bravo!"

Mr. Wagner, in cowboy boots and a ten-gallon hat, was caller for the third- and fourth-grade square dances. Suzie said, "Boy, Mr. Wagner would be good in a Western movie! He doesn't look old at all today."

During the relay races, touch ball, and volleyball, Co Co roared, "Bravo! Bravo!" But in the baseball game between the fifth- and sixth-grade boys, she screamed, "Don't walk him—don't walk him—you knucklehead!" just as if she'd been on an American playground all of her life.

When the music started for the Maypole dances, Suzie and Co Co gathered up the kindergartners again and kept a weather eye peeled for trouble. To their amazement the little ones clutched their ribbons and wound in and out without a single mistake. Then the first, second, third, fourth, and fifth grades followed. Each Maypole dance was a little more complicated than the last, and each was completed perfectly.

The sixth-grade dance was the most difficult of all. They knew their routines and everything would have been just fine, had Bravo not appeared and joined in.

When Rich saw him he said, "Gosh, I'll bet the window was open!"

Bravo barked and wound around their legs. He bit the ribbons and tried to play tug-of-war. Before the Maypole was half wound up, the sixth grade was in such a tangle they appeared to be binding one another to the stake. Miss Morrison tried to help them, but she, too, gave up as wave after wave of laughter swept the audience.

The sixth grade obviously couldn't move, let alone finish the dance, so Mr. Wagner announced over the loudspeaker that if the graduating class would stand still, he would like to have everyone join in the farewell song.

All year long Suzie had been dreading this sad part of the May Day program. She was afraid she might break down and cry and disgrace her class and her mother. Just as the song reached the saddest part— "We're proud of you—And we've seen you through . . ." Bravo sat down, threw back his head and howled like a wolf.

Rich and Ray tried to stop him and in the process, tipped over the Maypole, and pulled everybody to the ground. As a result, instead of being sad, the sixth grade received their final salute, giggling and looking more like an old trampled football pompon than a proud graduating class.

They were still heaving and struggling to get free when the audience poured onto the playground to congratulate them for the program. Millicent was the first to jerk herself loose. With one disdainful look and, "Honestly, I'm so ashamed I could die!" she rushed across the playground and disappeared.

It was time to set the tables for the banquet. Suzie and Co Co were counting chairs when Miss Morrison stopped them. "Have you girls seen Millicent? I've asked everyone else. She has the list for the seating arrangements, and I can't seem to find her."

They searched in the halls and in all the rooms and in the bathrooms and in the cloakrooms. "Do you think Millicent was so ashamed she went home?" Co Co asked.

Suzie shook her head. "She wouldn't dare. She's in

charge of seating, and the graduating class always stays right on the school grounds. We'll just have to start at the top of the building and look again. If we don't find her, we'll have to put the place cards around by ourselves, and then she'll really be furious."

When they finally found Millicent, it was so late the mothers and fathers were beginning to arrive. She was crouched down behind the galoshes rack in the third-grade cloakroom, crying as if her heart would break.

"What on earth is the matter? Nobody cares if the Maypole got mixed up," Suzie said, and Co Co added, "Come, Millicent. Miss Morrison is waiting for you. It is time for the banquet."

Millicent just sobbed harder than ever.

Suzie tried again. "We all feel bad about leaving Maple Leaf, but we'll be together in junior high next year."

Millicent sobbed, "But that's just it. I won't be here. I have to go to California and live with my Aunt Millie."

Co Co knelt down and put her arms around Millicent. "My poor little one. You must travel. No wonder you cry."

Millicent buried her head on Co Co's shoulder and sobbed that her stepfather was a salesman and had to travel all the time and she had to go to school so she couldn't live with her mother and had to live with her aunts. "And Aunt Mabel, that's the one I live with here, is young and she isn't married and she works. She takes me to movies all the time and she lets me do what I want to, except I always have to be neat. She sp-poils me, I guess, and I just lo-o-ve her." Millicent began to cry out loud.

Suzie patted her and Co Co crooned, "My poor little one—my poor little one."

Suzie, whose eyes were wide with imagined whippings and diets of bread and water, asked breathlessly, "Is your California aunt cruel to you?"

Millicent shook her head. "No, she's nice but she's used to children. She makes me go to bed early and won't let me wear lipstick or call up boys, and I know I'll just *hate* it! She has three boys of her own and they tease me and call me 'sissy'!"

Co Co winked at Suzie over Millicent's head. "How fortunate for you. The boys will bring other boys . . ."

Suzie chimed in. "Yes, and you'll have more dates and everything."

Millicent sat up and began to wipe her eyes. "Why, I never even thought of that." She stood up and looked in the mirror and wailed, "I *can't* go. I look just awful and everybody will know I've been crying."

Suzie said, "No, they won't. I'll get you a wet towel and a comb and you'll look just lovely. You always look pretty—just like a movie star. No wonder all the boys like you best."

To their amazement, Millicent burst into loud sobs again. "They—do—not! My aunt Mabel wants me to look cute and says no wonder all the boys are crazy about me, but they *aren't*." She turned and looked at them with brimming eyes. "Promise you won't tell a soul if I tell you something? Cross your hearts?" They both promised. "I've never had a single date in my life!"

Co Co and Suzie swallowed and tried not to look too cheerful as they exclaimed together, "You haven't!"

"No-o-o-o!" Millicent bawled so loudly that they thought she could probably be heard clear down in the lunchroom.

Suzie said briskly, "Millicent, you're chairman of the seating arrangements. Not one soul can sit down until you bring the list."

Millicent sobbed louder, "I do-o-o-n't c-a-a-r-e."

Co Co said, "I hope you do not let your tears fall on the beautiful silk frock."

Millicent turned her tears off just like a faucet and fluffed up her skirt. "My aunt sent me this dress from California and it's real silk. I'm the only girl in our room who has a silk dress." She washed her face and combed her hair and said, in her regular bossy voice, "Well, what are we waiting for? You seem to forget, after all, that I'm chairman of the seating." With that she switched out of the cloakroom.

All the way to the lunchroom, she gave them advice

on how to behave at the banquet. As she put down the place cards, she whispered in code, waved and giggled at the boys, and ordered the girls around.

Co Co whispered, "Pouf—she is still a beast!" and Suzie added, "I just hope her California aunt is good and cruel to her."

But in spite of Millicent, the banquet was a great success. The parents complimented the children extravagantly when they gave the toasts to the class. Mr. Wagner made a graduating speech, which was full of jokes and teasing personal remarks. Co Co kept murmuring to Suzie, "The banquet—it is indeed neat!" The food was perfectly delicious and everybody had a good time.

On the way home they talked the whole day over. Suzie said, "Really, May Day was just neat—it was the neatest ever! There is only one thing—I keep thinking about Millicent and wondering if she lived with her mother, maybe she wouldn't act so sappy."

Co Co shrugged. "I am afraid not. It is the boy crazy which makes Millicent appear gauche. Mademoiselle was right. A young girl should be polite and courteous to boys, but she should not call them on the telephone and run after them. You and I like Rich and Ray the best, but we are not boy crazy and we will never, never behave like Millicent."

Chapter Nine

The Lookout

Saturday morning when Suzie and her mother came down to breakfast, it was raining hard. Gusts of wind whipped the garden and blew the yellow rosebush against the kitchen window until the petals stuck on the panes like little yellow faces begging to come in.

Suzie's mother said, "I'm sorry it's raining. I'd like to think of something amusing to do with you and Co Co, but I promised Mr. Langdon I'd help him get some things for his house."

"Think nothing of it," Suzie said as she served breakfast. She brought the blueberry muffins and sausages and scrambled eggs over to the table. "Co Co and I wouldn't have been able to go with you anyway because we're going to play pioneer. We've been just waiting for a blustery day, and personally I hope there's a regular cloudburst."

Suzie's mother smiled. "That sounds like fun. I probably won't be home until late because we're going to dinner and the theater."

Suzie licked the buttery muffin off her fingers. "That's good. I'd feel awfully selfish leaving you alone so many Saturdays if it weren't for Mr. Langdon. It's a good thing there's a Langdon for each of us because I'd planned to eat dinner at Co Co's, but she said she'd rather have dinner here and stay all night and go to Sunday school."

Suzie's mother said, "You may do as you like about it, but don't forget to take my slicker for Co Co. I doubt if she has one."

Suzie giggled. "She'll call it a 'sleeker' and wrinkle her nose and say 'eet smells fonnee.'"

While Suzie was talking she was scurrying around, clearing off the table, making a lunch to take to the Lookout, and stacking the breakfast dishes. When she was ready, she kissed her mother good-bye and said, "Have a good time and don't worry about us. We'll be coming over the Cascades in a covered wagon." She whistled to Jet and ran across the orchard, yoo-hooing to Co Co.

When she climbed up into the Lookout, there was Co Co crouched under an enormous black umbrella.

Suzie handed Co Co the slicker, whereupon Co Co put it on and said, "You call it a sleeker. Hmmm—it smells fonnee."

Suzie giggled and unrolled the canvas hood and pulled it over their heads and fastened it down. Meanwhile Co Co was struggling to fold the enormous umbrella. "This is Mademoiselle's umbrella. I hate it, but she would be angry in Paris if I allowed the rain to fall on me. There, it did not pinch my finger today. Oh, you have the picnic. Me, I have one also. Excellent! Now, let us begin. It is a dar-r-rk night—we are alone under the tree—we have a bed of leaves. It is cold and we shiver-r-r! We have been gathering sticks. While we are gone, the Indians come and scare our maman and papa, and they must go without us. This man is crawling toward us. Perhaps, he will capture one of us and take her with him on his horse—saddle."

Sometimes Suzie felt that Co Co was almost too good at playing pioneer. She shivered and said, "But the pioneers wouldn't be so careless as to run off and forget their children, would they?"

"Oh-ho, but they did. We are cold, and hungry, and so frightened! We see his head feather sticking out, and we do not take a breath. *Now*—he leaps and snatches me from beside you. He puts me on his horse saddle and gallops away. I bite him and kick him and scream and cry—but he laughs and rides through the night—far, far away. Now, Suzie, you are all alone in the dar-r-r-k forest! You cry and cry—but no one hears you but the sighing trees. The wolf is licking his lips! What do you do?"

Gooseflesh crawled along Suzie's arms and her heart thudded as she listened to Co Co's hushed, scary voice. "Gosh, you'd better let me think while you tell me what happened to you when the Indian stole you."

As this was exactly what Co Co was waiting for, she settled back and told a hair-raising story of being captured. When she turned into a beautiful Indian princess and began to lead the pioneers through a pass in the mountains, Suzie sat up. "Listen, Co Co—you can't be Sacajawea. I told you about her and I dibs her."

Co Co giggled. "You asked me where I go. I told you. But now, I cannot walk so far without the lunch." She poured two cups of hot cocoa and handed one to Suzie with a sandwich. "So—you are alone under that tree. You must tell me another pioneer story, or I will leave you there until you are nothing—little dry, white bones—peelings!"

Suzie shuddered. "I don't know whether it's the rain on the leaves or what, but today, playing pioneer gives me the creeps. Let's play movie star. I choose a pure white dress with diamonds all over the top and dripping down the skirt and diamonds all over the toes of my slippers and . . ."

It was five o'clock when Suzie stretched and said, "Gosh, I'm stiff. Let's get your suitcase and go home."

Co Co spoke slowly, eyeing Suzie. "I wish to ask

you something. Would you allow me to have half of the Lookout?"

Suzie gulped and didn't answer for a minute. The Lookout was her own special place, and she'd never thought of sharing it with anyone, but Co Co's face was so eager and her eyes were shining with excitement, so Suzie said hastily, "Sure. We'll divide up the cupboards and I'll ask Grandfather to have another key made, and . . ."

Co Co threw her arms around Suzie. "Oh, my Suzie, you are the dearest friend in all the world. Now, I will give you half of my swimming pool and the pink bedroom. They are not as delightful as the Lookout, but they are all I have to give to you."

The lights were on in Grandfather's toolshed as they sloshed their way through the orchard. Suzie stopped and called, "Grandfather, let us in. I want you to have another key made for Co Co, for her share of the Lookout. Grandfather?"

Grandfather opened the door a crack. "Sorry, chickens, I have a surprise in here and nobody can come in." He closed the door and the electric saw started to buzz again.

Suzie said, "I'll bet it's something for our birthdays." She peeked in the window. "He's just sawing boards."

Co Co jerked the hem of Suzie's slicker. "We must not look. I found my Christmas present in Paris and

Papa was stern. He said an American child does not hunt for presents."

They opened the kitchen door and found Grandmother basting a chicken. The kitchen was warm and smelled deliciously of stuffing and gravy. Co Co took one look at the crisp, brown bird and said, "Chicken! Ummm! It is my favorite!"

Suzie said, "Me, too!"

"Now scoot upstairs and take off those wet things and put on your pajamas and bathrobes," Grandmother said. "We'll pretend it is the dead of winter and have supper in front of the fire in the living room."

They took hot baths and came downstairs in their bathrobes, their faces shining and their cheeks pink and their hair plastered down so it looked like varnished wood. Grandfather built a roaring fire in the fireplace and Grandmother served roast chicken, spoonbread, apple and celery salad, and hot tea. The girls ate as though they had really been lost in the woods, until Grandmother reminded them not to forget dessert. She brought in a chocolate pie with meringue like drifts of golden snow.

Then Co Co and Suzie popped corn and toasted their toes.

Grandfather said, "I thought we might take a trip to Eastern Washington this summer and watch them round up some wild horses in horse heaven."

"Horse heaven?" Co Co's eyes were black with excitement. "Is it true? Is this the wild horse of the Indian? Suzie told me, but I thought it was long, long ago."

Grandfather said there were still great bands of wild horses and Indians, too, for that matter. He said the Indians were friendly and were the first true Americans, but they were forced to live on reservations. He suggested that as soon as school was over, the girls should sleep out in the orchard in their sleeping bags, to practice for the camping trip.

The telephone rang and they both rushed to answer it. Suzie almost dropped the receiver when she recognized Ray's voice and heard him say, "Hey, Suze—this is Ray. Guess what? Bravo's lost."

Suzie blushed crimson and asked questions until Co Co was nearly beside herself with curiosity. "What is it? Who is on the telephone? What is it?"

Suzie said, "Just a minute—here she is," and handed the receiver to Co Co. "Rich wants to speak to you."

It was Co Co's turn to blush as she said, "Clothilde Langdon speaking. Who is on the telephone?" She giggled. "Oui, oui, it is also Co Co." She nodded and frowned and made gestures in the air with her right hand. This time it was Suzie's turn to hop up and down and ask questions. Co Co shook her head. "You talk to him. I cannot understand. He speaks of the park."

Suzie talked some more, giggled and said, "Okay. See you tomorrow." She turned to Co Co. "Gosh, I almost died. This is the very first time a boy ever called me up. Anyway, they said Bravo's lost and they've looked everywhere for him. They're coming over after Sunday school to get us so we can help hunt for him. I hope Bravo hasn't been run over or something."

Co Co yawned. "Let us go to bed."

Chapter Ten

A Rainy Date

Sunday morning, Suzie and Co Co hurried home from Sunday school and began to change into their jeans and sweaters so they would be all ready when Rich and Ray arrived.

Co Co looked in the mirror and shook her head. "We do not appear chic. I would like to appear attractive with Rich and Ray."

Suzie said, "Heavens to Betsy! After all, they're just *boys*!"

The doorbell rang and Suzie almost knocked Co Co down in her rush to answer it.

Rich and Ray wore dripping yellow slickers and hats and waterproof boots. Rich said, "Better wear your slickers. It's raining cats and dogs."

Suzie's mother called out and asked them when they thought they would be back.

Ray said, "We've got enough money for lunch and stuff. We might not get back until six o'clock, if that's all right with you, Mrs. Green."

Co Co muttered, "The sleeker—it smells fonnee," but she put it on, and they started out in the rain, whistling and calling for Bravo.

When they passed Mrs. Medlin's hedge, Ray said, "You don't suppose Old Medler Medlin has Bravo locked up or something, do you?"

Suzie shook her head. "Uh-uh. If she ever found him she'd have a fit and personally take him to the pound."

They exchanged all sorts of stories of Mrs. Medlin and her dangerous qualities, while they hunted around the school and in every alley and street nearby.

When they got to the park, Rich suggested that he and Co Co take one set of paths and Ray and Suzie the other, in order to cover the park more quickly. Trees dripped down their necks, branches caught at their arms, and vines tripped them. They met over and over again at the crossings, but there wasn't a sign of Bravo.

It was two o'clock when they came back to the entrance for the third time. Their faces were streaked with dirt, their jeans were torn, and they were all soaking wet and discouraged.

"I slid down a bank into a darned old ditch and got

mud all over me." Rich kicked his toe against the curb.

Co Co patted his arm sympathetically. "But you were brave when you were hurt. Perhaps if we had a hamburger, we would have a new spirit. I am always sad when I am hungry."

Rich brightened immediately and they trudged across the street to a restaurant. The bright lights, the music from the jukebox, and the smell of sizzling hamburgers cheered them up so much, they began to laugh at one another's woeful appearance.

Co Co said, "If you will excuse us, we will comb our hair and wash our faces, and then we will eat and eat."

When they came back, Rich and Ray had also washed their faces and combed their hair, and Rich had ordered four jumbo hamburgers and four chocolate malted milks. He grinned at Co Co. "You sure are an expensive date, Appetite."

While they were eating, Co Co suggested such frightening possibilities as to Bravo's whereabouts, that Rich and Ray were struck dumb with admiration. Suzie, however, was concentrating on what Rich had said to Co Co. "You're an expensive *date!*" If Co Co began to have dates with Rich, she wouldn't want to pretend in the Lookout, or take camping trips, or anything else. Suzie sucked violently on her straw, made a loud gurgling noise, and blushed.

Ray said, "Take it easy, Gurgles. Gurgles Green—pretty neat!"

Suzie said, "Don't you dare call me that at school."

Ray changed the subject. "Say, what if the FBI picked Bravo up and are using him for a tail?"

Co Co looked puzzled. "What is it—the FBI? Why do they wish to use Bravo's tail?"

Rich explained that the FBI was sort of a detective agency for the American government and that the word *tail* meant sort of like being a shadow.

Co Co laughed and said she had seen the FBI in the cinema and was a dumb, dopey knothead to forget.

Rich patted her hand. "You're plenty sharp, chum—plenty! After all, Ray and I wouldn't ask you and Suzie for our first dates if you were a couple of dummies, would we?"

Suzie looked so startled that Co Co said, "Is this then—*a date*?"

"What else? You are the only girls we could think of who'd want to hunt for good old Bravo. Isn't that so, Ray?" Ray agreed.

Rich and Ray got up and went over to pay the check. While they were gone, Co Co leaned over and flicked Suzie's chin with her fingertip. "You try to hide, but I see the twinkle in the eye. The date is pleasant, n'est-ce pas?"

Chapter Eleven

A Moonlight Adventure

In spite of the beautiful weather, the last week of school was discouraging. All day long they had final examinations; then, after school, they spent most of their time hunting for Bravo. To be sure, Millicent had gone, and Rich and Ray walked as far as Mrs. Medlin's gate with them every day, which should have been exciting, but they never talked about anything but Bravo, who was still lost.

They talked so much about Bravo that Mr. Langdon offered to take them all down to the Humane Society on Thursday after school, to see if there was any report down there.

The children were surprised to find the pound a very pleasant place, instead of a grim dog jail. The manager was friendly and showed them the indoor and outdoor kennels, the dog surgery, the ambulance, and all of the dogs and cats and birds.

Ray whispered to Suzie, "I notice he doesn't show us the dogcatcher. I'll bet he's an old meanie!"

The manager smiled at Mr. Langdon and said to Ray, "How would you like to meet a dogcatcher?" He opened a door and introduced a pleasant, blond young man who was stroking a golden Labrador and watching her feed her fat cream-colored puppies.

Suzie exclaimed, "Why he doesn't look very cruel!" Then clapped her hand over her mouth.

The dogcatcher laughed. "I'm *not* cruel," and handed a puppy to each of the children to hold.

Co Co, who had been asking her father for each dog, as she passed the various kennels, said, "Oh, Papa, please may I have this puppy for my birthday? May Suzie and I each have one?"

The dogcatcher said, "Goldie's puppies are only three weeks old, and they have to stay with her for a while."

Rich and Ray were stroking their puppies and looking wistful. "We'd sure like to have them. Golden Labs are the best hunting dogs of all, but gee, we already have two dogs and when we find Bravo, we'll have him, too. But gee, we could ask our parents!"

They played with the puppies a little while longer. Suzie wanted to name hers "Creamy" and Co Co named hers "Blonde," while Rich and Ray decided on "Sport" and "Pal." They reluctantly returned the puppies to the worried mother and with many longing, backward looks, left the pound.

The next day, instead of offering to walk home from school with them, Rich and Ray didn't even say good-bye. They just rode off on their bikes.

"Well, I like that! They might have at least told us." Suzie linked her arm in Co Co's and they started morosely down the street. "I'll bet if the rest of the kids would help us hunt, we'd have Bravo back by tonight. Rich keeps saying, 'Relax, chum, relax!' He makes me sick!"

Co Co flared up. "Suzie! Do not speak rudely of Rich. He is my friend!"

Suzie jeered, "Boyfriend, you mean. You sound to me like you're boy crazy! Go ahead and join the Select Seven. See if I care."

Co Co said, "Suzie Green—shut up!"

"Shut up yourself!" Suzie shouted.

With their noses in the air, they walked the rest of the way home on opposite sides of the street. It was their first quarrel, and although they were both almost crying, they didn't even speak as they converged at Suzie's back door and came in the kitchen together.

Co Co dumped her books on the table. "Grand'mère! Name of a name! I know nothing—my head is empty. In the morning, I write down *what I do not know* for

Mademoiselle Morrison. She reads what I write and shakes her head. In the afternoon I go to Monsieur Wagner's office. He talks to me—I forget the English—and he also shakes his head. I cannot go to the big school next year."

Grandmother sighed. "Well, tomorrow's the last day and there's no use crying over spilt milk. Next year it will all be different in junior high school."

Suzie whined, "Yes, and I'll bet those stuck-up kids won't even speak to us!" She looked mournfully out the window. "I honestly don't think I'd mind so much if we could just find Bravo."

Grandmother looked at the two sad, turned-down mouths, and racked her mind for something to cheer them up. "Bravo is probably hunting pheasants and sleeping in the park. Speaking of sleeping, why don't you get your sleeping bags and have a campfire in the orchard and cook dinner and sleep outdoors?"

"Grandmother, what a neat idea!" They immediately forgot they were fighting, rushed upstairs, and got the sleeping bags. Then they spent the rest of the afternoon setting up a tarpaulin between the trees and building an elaborate camp in the orchard. Grandfather built them a fire in the firepit, and then sat down and told them stories until Grandmother called him in for dinner.

After Co Co and Suzie had finished their outdoor supper, they sat around the campfire, toasting marshmallows and singing songs. When it was dark they crawled in their sleeping bags and told ghost stories and scary movies until they were jumping at every noise in the orchard.

The moon came up and made a shaft of silver on the lake; it touched the blossoming trees with pale fingertips. Co Co said, "Let us sleep in the light of the moon. Mademoiselle would never allow it. She said it makes one deranged." So they put their feet under the tarpaulin and lay watching the moonlight until they went to sleep.

It was almost midnight when something awoke Suzie. At first she didn't know where she was, and then she began to hear crackling noises and see weird shadows. That was nothing. It was only the wind blowing the leaves and causing them to rustle. She moved farther down into her sleeping bag. What was that? The tall pine—it always creaked and groaned. She reached her hand out and felt for Jet's warm, familiar back. Jet wasn't there. She swallowed and lay stiff as a board, listening and watching.

Something gleamed at the bottom of the orchard! She held her breath as she watched a shadow slip from tree to tree. The moonlight caught it, and Suzie saw that it was a big silvery animal! She shook Co Co. "Wake up! Wake up!" Suzie was so frightened she stuttered. "It's a b–b–ig d–d–og or w–w–olf!"

Co Co sat up and rubbed her eyes.

Suzie grabbed her shoulder. "Look! Over there by Mrs. Medlin's hedge. A big gray dog!"

The dog came running lightly through the trees, stopped, and stood over them, panting.

"Suzie, I believe it is Bravo!"

"He can't be. This one has short hair and he's all shiny!"

"But it is Bravo! It is Bravo with his hair gone!" Co Co patted the dog and he gave a yelp of welcome and licked both their faces, his stubby tail wagging his whole body. It was Bravo all right, but he looked funny and acted very peculiarly. He kept whining and running off a little way, then coming back to them and whining again.

Suzie said, "He wants us to follow him. Jet always acts like that when he wants something. Come on." They put on their bathrobes and slippers and followed Bravo across the moon-shadowed orchard.

When they reached Mrs. Medlin's hedge, Bravo wriggled through and barked.

"Shhh! You must not go in the garden of the wicked witch." Co Co snapped her fingers and Bravo came back and whined and then disappeared through the hedge again.

Suzie said, "He'll wake the whole neighborhood. Come on, we'll have to go around by the gate and see what he wants."

Just as they reached the corner, they heard a faint cry from the direction of the Tower House. Co Co clutched Suzie. "What was that?" The cry was repeated again; this time it was long and drawn out, thin and wailing. Bravo began to bark.

"We've just got to go in there before Mrs. Medlin comes roaring out and shoots Bravo." Suzie opened the gate and they tiptoed down the path. She whistled softly and Bravo appeared beside her. Then he ran to the back door and stood there whining.

Co Co said, "Suzie, do not go. I am afraid! Mrs. Medlin's house is a witch's castle—look!"

Suzie shivered, partly because of Co Co's scary voice, but mostly because the house *did* look like a witch's castle. The turrets, outlined against the moon, were tall and black. The windows were like black, staring eyes, and the balconies cast weird shadows. A bush scraped against a window with a little screech; Co Co screamed and Bravo hurled himself against the kitchen door and barked furiously. They heard a cry of "Help, help! Ohhhh—help!"

"Suzie, it is a ghost! Quick, quick!" Co Co grabbed Suzie's bathrobe and almost pulled it off.

"Shhhh! Co Co, don't be silly. A ghost wouldn't cry for help and anyway, that sounds like Mrs. Medlin. Come on, we'll have to see what's the matter, even if she gets so mad she calls the girl-catcher."

Ordinarily, Suzie wouldn't have thought of wandering around in the dark trying to rescue people, but Co Co was so terrified that she felt she had to be brave. She walked up and rattled the back doorknob and rang the bell. Then she led the way around to the front of the house, rang the bell and pounded on the door. This time they heard a distinct cry—"Help, help! Please, help!"

"You are right, Suzie. It is not a ghost. We must get in the house. Quick, quick!"

They tried the door and then one window after another. Meanwhile Co Co was muttering, "I hope it is Mrs. Medlin. I hope it is not an assassin who will chase us with the knife."

Suddenly Bravo disappeared right in front of them. Suzie leaned down to see where he had gone. "It's a low cellar window. I've got a flashlight. I'll go first and you follow me." She flashed her light around and saw the open window. "We'll probably have to jump, but I think we can make it." She stepped down, crawled through the window, hung by her hands, and let go. There was a loud *crash!* She called, "Come on. I landed on a few paper cartons, but I didn't hurt myself."

Co Co dropped down beside her and they sneaked through the dark basement, Suzie's flashlight winking ahead of them. It shone on rows and rows of barrels and Co Co stopped. "Suzie, do you think Madame

Medlin is another Barbe Bleu—the gentleman with the blue beard? Perhaps she puts the children and dogs she finds in her garden in the barrels!"

They began to giggle, partly because of the strain and partly because Co Co always thought up such scary things. Again they heard the cry for help. Bravo barked and came back to them, and they followed him up the basement stairs. Suzie flashed her light around until she located the light switch. They followed Bravo through the hall and up the stairs, and there, lying on the floor, was Mrs. Medlin.

"Oh Suzie, I—think—I've—broken . . ." Mrs. Medlin's voice faded. Her face was gray, her lips were white, and her right leg was lying at a peculiar angle.

"The leg! It is broken! You must call a doctor. I will get the blankets and a pillow!" Co Co ran into a bedroom and came staggering back under mounds of bedding. She tucked blankets around Mrs. Medlin, gently lifted the injured leg, and put a pillow under it. "She must not be cold, she will have the shock!"

Suzie said she would call her mother and Dr. Bell. She ran into Mrs. Medlin's bedroom and telephoned. "Hello, Mother? I'm at Mrs. Medlin's house and Co Co thinks Mrs. Medlin's leg is broken. Can you come over? Yes, I'm going to call the doctor right now." Then she called Dr. Bell and told him what had happened and asked him if he could come right away. Then she ran back and knelt down beside Mrs. Medlin, wiped her forehead with a handkerchief, and murmured, "Don't worry. Everything is going to be all right. Mother is coming and so is Dr. Bell."

Meanwhile Bravo was circling around and whining and nudging Mrs. Medlin with his nose. He licked her hand and dropped down beside her. Mrs. Medlin opened her eyes, smiled, and whispered, "How did you girls find me?"

Suzie said, "Bravo woke us up. We were sleeping in the orchard, and he barked and whined so much we just had to follow him."

Mrs. Medlin reached her hand out toward Bravo. "He is a—remarkable—dog." She closed her eyes. "I'm so cold. Did you say Dr. Bell was coming?"

Co Co tucked the blankets around her more firmly. "Do you think you could drink tea, Madame? It would make you warm." She said in a low voice to Suzie, "Perhaps if you could make some tea, we could give it to her until the doctor arrives."

Suzie ran down to the kitchen, put the kettle on, and began to hunt for the tea. Her mother knocked at the back door. "Darling? What on earth is the matter? How do you happen to be over here?"

"Oh Mother, help me! Mrs. Medlin has broken her leg, and we're trying to keep her warm until the doctor comes."

The kitchen door opened again and Dr. Bell came in, slapping his gloves together. On the way upstairs he said, "It's a good thing you heard her. I've been telling her for years something like this was liable to happen."

He examined Mrs. Medlin's leg, said it didn't look like a serious break, but he'd better call an ambulance and take her to the hospital and have it X-rayed. "It's a wonder it wasn't her hip," he grumbled as he went into the bedroom to telephone.

When he came back he told Suzie and Co Co that they were better than most adults in an emergency, and he certainly was proud of them. Then he suggested that they go downstairs and watch for the ambulance.

In no time at all, the big green ambulance drew up in front of the house. Suzie opened the door, and Co Co showed the men the way upstairs. The two girls watched with great interest as the men lifted Mrs. Medlin, put her on the stretcher, and carried her downstairs, as effortlessly as if she weighed no more than a powder puff.

Dr. Bell left, and Suzie's mother turned out all the lights and locked the back door. She said, "We'll take Bravo home with us, and I'll give all of you some hot milk. Also, I'd like a coherent picture of just what happened tonight."

Bravo, however, had other ideas. When they started up the street, he turned and went back to Mrs. Medlin's back porch, heaved a large sigh, and settled down.

Suzie called and whistled but Bravo wouldn't follow. She giggled. "I'll bet he thinks we called the lady-catcher for Mrs. Medlin. After all, the ambulance is a green truck."

Chapter Twelve

Suzie Has a Good Idea

The next morning was the last day of school. The class filed into the room and sat down to wait for their report cards. Over the whispering, pushing, giggling, and general air of vacation, Miss Morrison asked if anyone had an interesting experience to tell the class while she checked in the books.

Suzie and Co Co both raised their hands, Miss Morrison nodded, and Suzie began:

"Last night Co Co and I put up the tent in the orchard and cooked our supper outdoors and slept in sleeping bags. We'd been asleep for ages, and it was pitch dark except for the moon, when something woke me up. . . ."

Co Co broke in, "The moonlight makes dark shadows. We are so frightened we cannot speak. We hear strange sounds. From behind the tree a big, silvery animal comes creeping toward us. His eyes shine in the dark! He creeps along like this—" Co Co crept up the aisle, snarling and sniffing.

Suzie hooted like a faraway owl. "And we heard this moaning sound, kind of like an owl only more like a wolf. This silvery animal looked like a wolf, too. We were just scared to death! Then the moaning started up again and it seemed to come from Old Medler Medlin's—I mean Mrs. Medlin's garden. . . ."

"We fear it is an assassin with a big knife, who will cut us while we sleep. . . ."

"But it wasn't. It was a big gray dog. . . ."

"Bravo! You found Bravo!" Rich and Ray shouted. "Where did you find him? Where is he? Did you lock him up?"

The rest of the class, who had been watching Suzie and Co Co in open-mouthed amazement, all began to shout at once.

Miss Morrison held up her hand for silence. "Let us allow them to continue their adventure."

So Suzie told the story, and Co Co furnished the dramatic action. Finally Suzie said, "Well, that's just about all, except we can't figure out why Bravo thinks he lives with Mrs. Medlin."

Ray asked, "Yeah, but who's feeding him?"

"We are, but he won't leave Mrs. Medlin's yard, so we have to feed him over there. It's the most mysterious thing we've ever heard of."

Miss Morrison walked up and down the aisles distributing the report cards. Co Co watched each child jerk open his brown envelope and listened to the groans of despair or crows of joy, depending on the grades. Her face got whiter and whiter as she sat with folded hands, looking just as scared as she had the first day she came to school.

At last Miss Morrison stopped by her desk and handed her a white envelope. Co Co swallowed and murmured, "Merci," but she did not open it.

Suzie leaned over and whispered, "Open it—open it! I just know you passed."

Co Co shook her head. "I cannot open it here."

The dismissal bell rang, and Miss Morrison put her hand on Co Co's shoulder. "Good-bye. I hope you all have a happy and delightful summer vacation. Next year, in French class, I want you to remember to call me Mrs. Wagner."

There was a dead silence as they tried to imagine Miss Morrison teaching French *and* married to a principal! Then there was a chorus of "Good-bye, Miss Morrison"s, and school was over.

As Suzie and Co Co walked down the steps of Maple Leaf School for the last time, Co Co said, "Oh, Suzie, I love the American school. So happy, so friendly, so charming," and Suzie said, "I'm glad it's over, but I'm sad, too—kind of. I'm sure glad I got all A's. Come on, Co Co—open your letter. I want to see what you got."

Co Co's hands were trembling so, she could barely get the white envelope open. Her lips moved as she read the letter through twice, very slowly. "Suzie, I think I passed also! Here, you read it and tell me."

Suzie read:

This is to certify that Clothilde Langdon has been examined and has completed the requirements to enter the seventh grade. —R. Wagner

She gave a shout of joy. "Sure. This is the same as a report card only you weren't here long enough to get a regular one. Oh, Co Co, isn't that neat? We both passed. Hooray! Hooray! Next year junior high!"

They ran all the way home and burst in the back door shouting, "Hooray, hooray, we've passed! We *both* passed! We've graduated! No more school! Hooray, hooray!"

Grandmother kissed them, said there had been no doubt in her mind that they would pass, and added that she had two surprises to celebrate the end of school. "The first one is really a surprise! Mrs. Medlin has asked both of you to lunch. And the second is,"—she opened the oven door and showed them a big, fat turkey—"Co Co and her father are coming for dinner!"

Co Co clapped her hands. "Oh, Grand'mère! I like turkey best of all! How good it looks! Ummmm!"

Grandmother patted her head. "Now suppose you skip up and put on your new plaid dresses."

When they came downstairs, they looked as neat and prim as if they were going to Sunday school. Grandmother handed them a big bouquet of flowers, a basket of fresh ginger cookies and some mystery books, and warned them not to stay too long because Mrs. Medlin wasn't strong yet.

They walked down the street hand in hand, whispering about how dangerous Mrs. Medlin was. Bravo was waiting at the gate. His curly topknot was tied with a pink ribbon, his bangs were brushed back out of his eyes, he wore a studded collar with a name plate, license tag, and identification disc hanging like charms from a bracelet. His back shone like hammered pewter, and his legs rippled like fox fur.

Suzie giggled. "Gosh! He looks just like a movie dog!"

Co Co said, "He is haughty also, like the poodles in Paris."

Bravo didn't even wag his tail. He turned and led them to the front door, gave one short peremptory bark, and the door was opened by a trained nurse who said, "Come in—come in. You must be Suzie and Co Co, those brave girls I've heard so much about." They followed the nurse up the stairs.

Mrs. Medlin greeted them in her usual cross voice. "Good morning. *Don't* sit on the bed. It makes me nervous as a witch. Not a wicked witch either." She gave a short bark of laughter, and Co Co jumped back, put her hand over her mouth, and blushed.

Suzie just stood and stared, she was so astonished at the change in Mrs. Medlin. She had always seen her dressed in grubby gardening clothes, but now she looked almost glamorous. She wore a pink frilly bed jacket, a pink ribbon tied around her short gray curls, pink lipstick and pink nail polish, and she had a pale-blue satin quilt tucked around her. But her voice hadn't changed as she snapped, "I want to thank you for rescuing me Friday night. I am extremely grateful. Amazing! Absolutely amazing! Someday I may be able to do something for you. In the meantime, please use my garden as if it were your own."

Suzie said, "Thank you," and Co Co said, "Merci, Madame." However, they both wondered if Mrs. Medlin realized how much like a cross teacher she sounded as she continued, "Please don't interrupt. When you arrived the other night, I had been trying to attract someone's attention for almost two hours. If it hadn't been for Bravo . . ." She snapped her fingers and said in an even crosser voice, "Come here, this instant."

To their astonishment, Bravo put his head on Mrs.

Medlin's bed and looked lovingly up at her. She snapped her fingers again. "Bravo, get in your basket. Good boy!"

Instantly Bravo went over and plopped down in the fanciest basket they had ever seen. It was white with a pink cushion, and beside it were twin dishes on a rubber mat, with "Water" stamped on one, and "Dinner" on the other. He closed his eyes in a bored way, put his head down on his paws, and went to sleep.

"That dog is remarkable! Absolutely remarkable!" Mrs. Medlin snapped. "He deserves a medal. When he saw that I was hurt, he tried to help me. Then when he found he couldn't help, he hunted all over the house until he found that basement window open. Bravo! Remarkable!" She leaned over and smiled down at Bravo, who didn't even bother to open his eyes.

Suzie gulped. "Bravo has always been smart. He . . ."

Mrs. Medlin held up her hand like a traffic policeman. "Please do not interrupt. I might just as well begin at the beginning." She put on large horn-rimmed glasses and glared at Suzie and Co Co until they wriggled.

"Saturday evening, I was listening to the ten o'clock news broadcast. I heard whining and scratching at the front door. I opened it and there was Bravo—a wetter, dirtier animal I have never seen. He had a frayed rope hanging from his collar. I said, 'Get out!' but he just stood there shivering and *smiled*. So, I took hold of the rope and literally dragged him through the kitchen and out into the garage. I must admit I had every intention of leaving him there until Monday morning and calling the Humane Society."

Co Co interrupted. "Oh, you must not . . ."

"Please do not interrupt. I had just climbed into bed, when that dog started to howl. He barked and howled until he almost drove me crazy. I opened the garage door, and a man was running down the path. Bravo dashed after him, barking every inch of the way. A prowler! And Bravo was trying to protect me!" Mrs. Medlin cleared her throat. "Remarkable! Then Bravo came back and whined and scratched on the door and, well, I let him right in the house!"

"The first thing Sunday morning, I tried to give him a bath. What a job! The bathroom was a sea of water, I was soaking wet, Bravo was patient, but it was obviously a job for a trained person. So I dried him off, put him in the car, and took him to a veterinary.

"The veterinary said Bravo was a good dog—half Kerry blue and half standard poodle, but he would look better if he were clipped. So, what with one thing and another, shots, toenails, clipping, the veterinary kept him there until Thursday evening. When I put him in the car, I just wish you could have seen him. Nobody has ever been as glad to see me in my life." She leaned over and said, "Bravo—good dog!"

Bravo sighed and rolled his eyes. Co Co chuckled and Suzie giggled. They tried to stifle their laughter, but it was no use. Mrs. Medlin started to say, "Don't interrupt" but changed it to, "Then I bought him this basket and his own dishes and made him understand that from now on he was to stay right beside me. I was about to show him his basket when I slipped on the rug and fell. Now. I've talked long enough and I daresay you're hungry." She rang the bell and asked the nurse to bring lunch.

When the nurse had left, she continued. "Before lunch, I have one more thing to say. Living alone makes people selfish—and lonely. Now that I have Bravo, I'm not lonely. It's a pleasant feeling. While we are having lunch, I want you to tell me all about yourselves."

So, while they ate chicken salad and hot rolls and ice cream and cake, they told Mrs. Medlin all about the Lookout, and Co Co's travels and what they did in school. At first they were a little shy, but she asked such understanding questions, and paid such strict attention, that they soon found her to be as interested and understanding as someone their own age.

It was almost five o'clock when the nurse came in and said Suzie's mother had called and reminded them it was time to go home. "Oh, I'm sorry," Suzie said. "We've had such a good time, we forgot all about tiring you."

Mrs. Medlin snapped, "Nonsense! I've had a most enlightening afternoon. I'm not in the least tired. I can hardly wait for you to come back and tell me more about Millicent and the Sappy Seven. Remarkable! Absolutely remarkable!"

Bravo accompanied them to the front gate, but he made no attempt to follow them and acted as if he could hardly wait to go back to Mrs. Medlin.

Grandmother had all of their favorite things for dinner. Turkey, crisp and brown, stuffing, mashed potatoes and gravy, and homemade strawberry ice cream. During dinner, they acted out their visit to Mrs. Medlin. Then they brought out Suzie's report card and Co Co's note, and Grandfather gave Suzie a dollar for each of her five A's, and Co Co five dollars because she did so well in school.

Co Co said, "And next year, Suzie and I will go to the big school, and I am to help the class with French. Is that not neat?"

Mr. Langdon cleared his throat and looked at Suzie's mother, as he said, "I don't think we'd better plan that far ahead. You know I must travel, and it will always be difficult for us to tell where we will be from one month to the next."

Suzie's heart sank. She watched her family give one another the "we'll discuss this later" look.

Mr. Langdon continued. "I, too, have a surprise for

smart girls. I have rented a cruiser, and tomorrow we'll pack a lunch and go through the Locks and cruise around Puget Sound. How would you like that?"

Co Co was immediately diverted and bounced up and down asking questions, first in French and then in English. Suzie, however, kept her eyes on her mother's face. She looked as if she were thinking about something sad as she said, "If you girls will clear off the table and stack the dishes, I'll do them later on."

Suzie caught part of a low-voiced conversation, as the grown people went into the living room. She picked up a plate and motioned to Co Co to pick one up also and tiptoed over to the doorway and stood listening.

Co Co's father said, "I'm fully aware of this, and I hate to disappoint her as much as you do, Helen, but I cannot leave Co Co here while I go to Mexico, and that job may take months. Boarding school seems the only solution."

Co Co clutched Suzie. "*Boarding school!* I will not attend. I will run away!"

They listened to snatches of a long argument. Grandmother and Grandfather and Suzie's mother all wanted Co Co to stay with them while her father was away. Mr. Langdon insisted that he couldn't impose on them to that extent.

Co Co became so upset that Suzie suggested that

they hurry and clear off the table and go to bed so they could talk.

After they'd finished stacking the dishes, they sneaked up the back stairs, undressed, and got into bed. Suzie tried to comfort Co Co with all the cheerful things she had ever heard about American boarding schools, but no matter how pleasant she tried to make them sound, big tears rolled down Co Co's cheeks and she kept repeating, "He promised me I would not have to travel anymore."

Finally Suzie asked, "What is a French boarding school like, anyway?"

Co Co sat up in bed. "Oh, Suzie, you do not know what Celeste, a French girl, told me. If the exercise book is not perfect, the teacher raps the hand. They are very strict. If the children are hungry, no one cares. At night they cry and cry and no one comes. Celeste said it was like a prison camp!" Co Co's eyes were black, as she remembered more and more things Celeste had told her. Co Co buried her head in her pillow and broke into a fresh storm of tears.

Suzie hunted around in her mind for even one comforting idea. Dorothy had been to boarding school once and she just loved it. She even cried when she had to go to Maple Leaf. Millicent had been to boarding school in California. Suzie gave a shout of joy. "Co Co, I've got an idea! Do you remember what Millicent said that day? 'If they're so crazy about each other why don't they get married?' Well, why don't they, and then you could stay here with me?"

Co Co sat up again and her eyes were shining. "Suzie! You are intelligent! What a wonderful idea!"

Suzie said, "The whole trouble is, how on earth do you make grown people get married?"

Co Co's eyes were dancing. "I know—wait—I believe I have an idea. In France, it is the custom to arrange the marriage. I do not know if I can tell you in English. Listen. In France, the mother and father choose the romance for the young people. In America, it is not the same thing. Here, the young lady is boy crazy and the young man is girl crazy and pouf—they get married! As in the cinema. In France, it is not the same at all—not at all."

Co Co held her head on one side and looked out of the corner of her eye. "In France, the love is not so important as the marriage. Mademoiselle has told me of this many times. One does not marry unless the families approve." She hugged her knees and rocked back and forth with the effort of translation. "I think this marriage could be arranged. Tell me, Suzie, are you fond of my papa?"

Suzie answered very seriously. "I just love him. He's awfully good looking and besides he's fun. He's really just neat! But the thing is, do you love my mother—

really, I mean—not just because she's mine?"

Co Co smiled. "Oh yes. She is beautiful and gentle and intelligent and so kind. Yes, I *do* love her."

Suzie said, "Okay. Then that's settled. Now, what do we do next?"

"We must make them feel that the marriage is necessary—a marriage of convenience. That they need one another, as we do."

Suzie hugged her knees and thought a minute. "You know something? Grandmother always says, 'That child needs a father,' every time I act smarty or whine or disobey."

Co Co interrupted, "And Mademoiselle told me constantly, when I misbehaved, that I was reflecting on the memory of my dear maman. Perhaps if we both behaved badly . . ."

There was a long silence. Suddenly Co Co jumped out of bed and rushed over to the dressing table and began hunting in Suzie's bureau drawers.

"What do you want?" Suzie got out of bed and stood beside her.

"Millicent! We will both be Millicents. Ah-ha, they will hate that and worry and worry and . . . Do you have the bobby pins?"

Suzie began to dance up and down. "Oh, Co Co, you have the best ideas in the whole world. Come on in mother's room. She has a whole box."

Chapter Thirteen

Boy Crazy

The next morning Suzie and Co Co got up before anyone else was awake and went down to the Lookout to complete their plans for the arranged marriage.

Suzie thoughtfully sucked an orange and gazed out over the lake as she listened to more of Co Co's ideas of the French arranged marriage. "Hey, wait a minute. Don't they even care whether they're in love?"

"Yes, it is well to have the twinkle in the eye and the sigh, but it is not important. The marriage must be necessary for the land, or the name, or the inheritance."

Suzie said, "Boy! It sure is necessary this time. You know, Co Co, in the movies, if grown-ups take a walk in the woods, even if they've been fighting like the dickens all day, they sit down under a tree and look into each other's eyes, and whamie—they're engaged!

Of course, if we worry them enough, they'll probably go off and talk about us."

"Oui, oui. The worry is begun with the bobby pins." Co Co pushed at her bangs, which were no longer smooth and shining, but stuck out like frizzy mattress stuffing.

Suzie giggled and patted her bangs, which looked like the inside of a cattail when it goes to seed. "Me, too. But remember, we also look like Millicent, and Mother never sees her that she doesn't shake her head and say, 'Suzie, I'm glad you don't feel you must look like Millicent.'"

Suzie began to jot down their ideas in her notebook. Co Co hung over her. "Do not forget the sad face—like this." She gazed at Suzie with wide grief-stricken eyes. "Oh, Papa, I wish I had a maman, beautiful and gentle, like Suzie's maman. Sometimes I feel as if I were the only child in America without a mother."

"Boy, that's neat! See if this is all right?" Suzie quivered her chin and cast down her eyes and looked tragic. "Mother, I hate to hurt your feelings, but it makes me feel so lonely and left out to watch Co Co playing with her father. I wish I had a father."

Suzie snapped her notebook shut. "I do hope they catch on. Grown-ups are pretty dense, especially about hints. Say, I know the 'Wedding March,' kind of. I'll play it whenever they're together."

"Excellent—excellent! You have good ideas, Suzie." Co Co checked off the items on her fingers. "The telephone, the lipstick, the bobby pin, the sadness, the wedding music. Oh, they will take the walk in the woods—they will have to."

They climbed down and ran back through the orchard. When they opened the back door, Suzie's mother and grandmother gasped simultaneously, "What on earth have you done to your hair?"

Co Co said, "The new coiffure—chic, is it not?" and Suzie added, "See, it's just like Millicent's. Isn't it cute?"

Suzie's mother sighed. "Oh dear, I suppose you must experiment but you looked so sweet with your straight hair and bangs. Come on, breakfast is all ready."

Co Co's voice was sickly sweet, as she asked, "Chère Maman, did Rich call me on the telephone?"

Suzie banged down her fork. "Gosh all fish hooks! They promised!" She giggled just like Millicent and whispered to Co Co.

All the time they were eating, they giggled and whispered and talked in code. Co Co winked at Suzie. "Oh, chère Maman, is it not neat? We have almost the steady with Rich and Ray!"

Grandmother snorted. "Going steady at your age! Of all the ridiculous . . ." she slapped another waffle down on Co Co's plate. "You'd better concentrate on that, young lady, and stop all this nonsense."

Co Co pushed at the waffle with her fork. "I do not think I can eat until Rich calls." She heaved a long, trembling sigh. "The romance—it is so wonderful!"

The telephone rang and they pushed and shoved each other in the race to answer it. Barbara was calling to see if they could go to a movie. Suzie mouthed, "It's Barbara," and then said in a high, silly voice, "Gosh, Ray, I thought you'd forgotten all about calling. Sure, we'd love to. Meet you at one o'clock. Don't forget now. Bye-e-e!"

She held down the shut off on the telephone and handed the receiver to Co Co. Co Co sounded exactly like Millicent as she cooed, "Rich, I've got something to tell you. Uh-huh. Uh-huh. No. You guess. Noooo! Well, I *do* like you best. See you later. Bye-e-e-e!"

They were delighted to hear Suzie's mother say, "Goodness, I didn't think they'd reach the silly stage for at least a year. I suppose it's that Millicent's influence."

Grandmother said, "As I've said before, Suzie needs a father and as for Co Co, goodness knows what will happen to that French imp without a mother!"

The girls hugged each other and sauntered back into the kitchen, arms entwined. Suzie said, "Mother, I thought I'd die. Ray said—oh-oh! I'd better not tell you."

Co Co simpered, "Four and five will take us to the

cinema this afternoon. We meet them at one o'clock."

Suzie's mother said, "But, girls, Mr. Langdon has hired the boat for this afternoon. You cannot disappoint him."

Co Co said airily, "You may go with him. I will tell him we also have the date. Come, Suzie, let us call up Rich and Ray and ask them to guess who this is."

Grandmother snapped, "You may not use my telephone to call up boys!"

Suzie's mother's voice was cool as she told them. "Please go upstairs and make the beds. Then you may come downstairs and clean the living room."

At noon, when Co Co's father walked in the door, there was a loud and inaccurate rendition of the "Wedding March," followed by hysterical giggles.

Suzie's mother said, "Girls, please go upstairs and get ready. The boat is waiting." They could hear her talking to Co Co's father in a low, worried voice, as they ran upstairs.

Co Co grinned at Suzie. "Let us put on the lipstick. Papa will be furious!"

Suzie drew a square Hollywood mouth with bright purplish-pink lipstick, and then called down in a high, silly voice, "We'll be right down, Daddy Bill, honey."

Co Co giggled. "Daddy Bill honey! Suzie, I am

indeed proud of you. We are hideous, but it is good. They will think so also."

They sauntered down the stairs, arm in arm, switching their pleated skirts and patting their frizzy hair. As they got to the bottom step, Co Co opened her purse, took out her mirror, and dabbed some powder on her nose. "Papa, I am sorry to disappoint you about the boat ride, but we cannot go. We have the date with Rich and Ray."

Before Mr. Langdon could speak, Susie's mother said, "Girls, please go right up stairs and wash your faces and comb your hair."

While they were still on the stairs, they heard Co Co's father say, "What is the meaning of this?"

Suzie's mother answered, "They're just copying one of the girls in school. I believe I can handle it."

This time they came down looking a little more natural, but still acting coy and silly. Co Co said, "Papa, would you be so kind as to drive us to the cinema? We will come home alone on the bus."

Mr. Langdon said, "Co Co, you know you are not allowed to ride busses alone."

Co Co shrugged, made a face, and began to hum "Speak to Me of Love" and to float around the front hall as if she were waltzing.

Suzie watched in open-mouthed admiration. Boy!

When Co Co decided to act boy crazy, she really did a good job!

She jumped guiltily as Mr. Langdon asked, "Suzie, what does this mean?"

Suzie turned wide, innocent eyes upon him. "What, Daddy Bill? Oh, nothing I guess, except that Co Co's just cra-a-a-zy about Rich and I'm just cra-a-a-zy about Ray." She began to sing, "I'm in Love with a Wonderful Guy" and dance with Co Co.

Suzie's mother snapped, "Suzie, behave yourself this minute!" and Co Co's father added, "Co Co, you are behaving outrageously!"

Co Co ran up and threw her arms around him. "Papa, oh Papa—do not be so cruel! If I had une chère maman, she would not allow you to be cruel to me. I wish *I* had a mother like Suzie." As she gazed up at her father, she looked exactly as if she were going to burst out crying.

Suzie's mother's eyes narrowed as Mr. Langdon immediately looked stricken. "Come, come now, ma petite. I didn't mean to sound cruel. You do not have to go on the boat. I thought you and Suzie would enjoy it, but you may go to the movie if you prefer to."

They kept up a constant stream of "he saids" and "I called hims" and giggled in Millicent's most infuriating manner, all the way down in the car.

When they arrived at the movie, most of their class was standing in line. Suzie said, "Rich and Ray are still waiting for us. Goodie, goodie!"

Co Co chimed in, "Quick, Suzie, see if my hair is right."

They self-consciously patted their frizzy curls, waved, and said, "Bye-e-e-e" and went to join the line.

Chapter Fourteen

Mrs. Medlin Comes to the Rescue

Monday afternoon, Suzie and Co Co were sitting by the pool, dabbling their feet in the water and having a council of war. "Honestly! I've been acting so corny—even impudent—and Mother acts just as if she didn't even hear me."

Co Co nodded morosely. "Me, also. I am so tired of the name of Rich. Papa laughs when I ask did Rich call me. He forgets that a courteous young lady would never, never call a young man on the telephone!"

The more they talked about their plans for the arranged marriage, the more discouraged they became. For three nights they had tossed and turned on stickery bobby pins. They had come downstairs in the morning with cross faces and hair that looked as if it had exploded. They had worn thick, Hollywood mouths with T-shirts, jeans, and tennis shoes.

Grandmother didn't even notice the giggling, whispering, and telephoning anymore. She even said, "My, I do hope that is Rich and Ray calling again. I was beginning to think we had a couple of old maids growing up around here."

As for Suzie's mother, she didn't pay one bit of attention. Just kept making lists and leaving the house right after breakfast to go shopping.

Suzie scowled and splashed the water with her feet. "Gosh! We might just as well give up and let them send you to boarding school!"

"Suzie, you do not care if I am cold and hungry!"

"I do, too, care. But you won't even try to count your blessings."

"Me, I have only one blessing. My papa."

"What about me? Aren't I a blessing? I always count you."

Co Co sniffed. "Yes, you are a blessing, but you have Grand'mère and Grand'père and your mother and Jet and three cats and . . ."

"For gosh sakes! You use them just as much as I do. Anyway, Grandmother already said you could have one of Smokey's kittens as soon as they're born. You're just feeling sorry for yourself."

They glared at one another and the fight was on.

They were both so cross and miserable that Suzie finally said, "It won't do us one bit of good to fight.

What if they did get married and we turned into sisters? Then they wouldn't even let us fight."

"Oh, no. Then we would quarrel much, much more. Sisters fight constantly. They scratch and bite and hit one another. It is terrible!"

For a while, Suzie became so interested in Co Co's harrowing tales of sisters' quarrels that she forgot all about her family's strange behavior. Then Co Co mentioned something about a birthday party she had attended, and Suzie said, "Say, that's another thing! Nobody has even mentioned our birthdays. Do you suppose they've decided that just because we're old enough for dates, we're too old for birthday parties? Gosh!"

Co Co shook her head. "I do not know."

They sat side by side, staring into the pool and brooding about difficult grown-ups. Suzie snapped her fingers. "Say, I'll bet Mrs. Medlin might have some ideas. Let's go and ask her."

"Suzie! You are indeed intelligent!" They jumped up and ran across the grass, jumped the hedge, and landed smack in the middle of Mrs. Medlin's best rhododendron bed.

Mrs. Medlin called out, "Careful!" but she waved to them and motioned for them to join her on the front porch. So they sat on the steps below her and she said, "Now, tell me every single thing you have been doing." They both talked at once and told her about the boarding school and the arranged marriage and how they had really been acting just awful and nobody seemed to care one bit.

Mrs. Medlin smiled once or twice, but she didn't interrupt. When they finally paused with a last, "Sometimes parents are just *awful!*" she nodded her head and said, "Yes, I agree with you. Sometimes parents are hard to understand."

She went on. "You want them to get married so Co Co won't have to go to boarding school. Now, I can't agree with you that boarding school is awful. I went to boarding school. Most fun I ever had. But the marriage seems like quite a good idea. Can't see one thing wrong with it. How do they seem to feel about it?"

Suzie said, "That's just it. We can't tell. Before we acted so awful, they were very polite to each other. Now they hunt furniture all the time."

Mrs. Medlin nodded. "Of course there is this. Had you thought of the fact that they might be afraid to get married now, because then each of them would have two badly behaved girls instead of one?" Mrs. Medlin smiled down into two pairs of stricken eyes and held up her hand like a traffic policeman. "Now, now, don't get upset. But if I were in your place, I'd stop pretending to be boy crazy, which sounds to me as if it was much more trouble than it's worth, and start acting natural. Suppose you go upstairs and shampoo your hair and then come down here and sit in the sunshine and let it dry so it shines the way it used to do. You'll find everything you need in the big bathroom closet."

When they came downstairs again, Mrs. Medlin said, "Now, let's forget all our troubles and talk about your birthdays. What kind of parties do you usually have?"

Co Co shook her head. "I have never had a birthday party. On my birthday, Papa asked the chef in our hotel to make a cake for me, and he invited guests with a child of my age."

Suzie interrupted. "I always have a party and Mother lets me invite as many children as I am old and one to grow on—like birthday candles."

"Well, suppose I give this birthday party for you. Were you planning to invite boys?"

Suzie said, "We'll probably have to now that we've acted so sappy. Everybody thinks we're boy crazy."

Co Co grinned. "And we are—a little."

Mrs. Medlin thought a minute. "Let's have the party on Saturday, the day between your birthdays, and invite the whole class." She smiled. "It's been so long since I had a birthday party. However, I'll talk to your parents. Now, if I were you, I'd go home and be sweet and helpful. I'd play all day in the Lookout or swim in the pool, or take walks with Bravo and Jet."

They thanked Mrs. Medlin and promised to come to see her every day, then ran home giggling, for the first time since Friday night.

They set the table and made the salad and helped in every way they could think of, and still their parents didn't seem to notice anything.

During dinner, Grandfather talked about the trip to Eastern Washington to see horse heaven. Co Co's father and Suzie's mother talked about the Pink House and furniture and wallpaper and dishwashers until Suzie whispered to Co Co that if her mother would act more like a movie star and less like a housewife, perhaps Mr. Langdon might want to sit under a tree with her.

All week long they did just as Mrs. Medlin suggested. They swam in the pool with Barbara and Dorothy and Sumiko. They rode their bikes with Rich and Ray. Every day they visited Mrs. Medlin and took Bravo for a walk. And they found that summer vacation had really begun, and they were having a wonderful time.

Monday morning the mailman brought each of them an invitation:

Mrs. Medlin is giving a party to honor the birthdays of
Suzie Green
and
Co Co Langdon

on Saturday, the 2nd of July, from five until ten.
Please bring bathing suits and jeans and sweaters and
tennis shoes.
R.S.V.P.

Co Co came tearing over to Suzie's house to compare notes. "Do you think she invited the whole class?"

Suzie said, "Gosh, I hope she remembered everybody. Let's call up and find out."

They were in the midst of calling everybody up, when Suzie's mother asked them if they would change their clothes and go shopping with her. Mr. Langdon had asked her to let them see his birthday presents a little early, to make sure they were right.

On the way downtown Suzie and Co Co both asked questions at once about Mrs. Medlin's exciting invitation.

Suzie's mother laughed and said she had promised on her word of honor not to tell them one thing about the party.

At the department store, they were wild with joy when the salesgirl brought out two party dresses with slippers dyed to match.

Suzie said, "Oh, Mother, pale green—and it's almost a short formal. Oh, isn't Mr. Langdon darling?"

Co Co exclaimed, "Yellow! It is lovely. Mademoiselle

would say I am too young to wear this frock, but Papa is behaving like an American. It is beautiful!"

They tried them on and stood side by side in front of the glass, admiring themselves. Suzie patted her full skirt. "Boy! I look almost grown up!"

Co Co giggled. "Rich prefers pink, but me, I prefer yellow. And the tight bodice with the tiny sleeve—very chic!"

The moment they got home, they rushed over to tell Mrs. Medlin about their new dresses, but the nurse said she was very busy talking to the caterer and some men about the lights.

When they rushed upstairs to tell Grandmother, she called out from her room, "Don't come in here. I have a surprise I don't want you to see."

They went out to the toolshed to tell Grandfather, but the electric saw was buzzing so loudly, they couldn't even make him hear.

They no longer had to pretend they were receiving telephone calls. The telephone rang every ten minutes! Rich and Ray and Johnny Allen and Sumiko and Marjorie and Barbara and Dorothy—the whole class called several times to compare notes.

Wednesday morning, Mrs. Medlin called and told them they must not come in the yard or even peek over the hedge.

Thursday, Mr. Langdon drove them downtown in

the morning, took them to lunch, and kept them there all day.

Friday morning, which was really Suzie's birthday, her mother took them to the beach to have a picnic. They dug clams and hunted agates and even took a quick dip in the ice-cold sound—anything to keep them from asking questions about the party.

When they got home, Suzie's mother said, "I'll have to leave the car out because Mrs. Medlin has a surprise in the garage."

Suzie wailed, "Oh Mother, you're just deliberately trying to torture us!"

Her mother grinned. "And Co Co is supposed to sleep here. Can't tell you why. Now, skip upstairs and get right into bed and go to sleep."

They did go right to bed, but they couldn't help whispering. Grandmother had to warn them five times to go to sleep.

Chapter Fifteen

Surprises

Saturday morning, Suzie woke up very early. She sang softly, "Oh, What a Beautiful Morning" as she looked out at the dazzling July sunshine. Grandmother's flower beds were a blaze of color. The distant mountains were dark blue. Glistening tufts of snow tipped their peaks and wound like silver ribbons down their valleys. The dark-green foothills were like a patchwork quilt with farms and orchards. The lake rippled with gold-tipped waves and the sun reflected arrows of light from the wings of the sea gulls, as they dipped and dove over the roof of the Pink House.

Suzie drew in a deep breath of summer air—cedar, salt water, and flower gardens. She hugged her knees and rocked back and forth, and smiled tenderly at her best friend, lying curled up in the other bed.

Co Co yawned and opened her eyes. "Happy

birthday, Suzie." She reached under her pillow and handed Suzie a little package.

Suzie reached under her pillow and handed Co Co a little package. "Happy birthday. Isn't it neat to wake up and find each other here?" They opened their presents to find identical friendship rings, which they put on their fourth fingers. "Now, let's hurry and get dressed and go down to the Lookout," Suzie said, excitedly. "Grandfather's present is down there. It always is."

They put on their jeans and T-shirts and tennis shoes and sneaked down the back stairs. They found a couple of cold muffins and two oranges, put them in their pockets, and ran across the orchard. When they reached the ladder, they found a large sign:

Surprise! Surprise!
Happy Birthday to my twins, Suzie and Co Co.
Love,
Grandfather

A big red arrow pointed in the direction of the big maple tree whose branches interlaced with those of the madroña tree. At the foot of the maple tree was another ladder and just visible at the top was another platform!

"Oh, Suzie, another Lookout!" They climbed the new ladder and sure enough, Grandfather had built

Co Co an exact duplicate of Suzie's Lookout. On top of the boxes was a big red sign: CO CO'S NEST. Hanging from the sign was an envelope in which were a silver chain and a key to the cabinets. "How magnificent! Cher Grand'père! My own nest!" Co Co was incoherent with excitement as she examined each cupboard. "A tent also and a hammock—and cushions! Oh Suzie, it is a Lookout, just like yours! Cher, cher, Grand'père! He knew how I longed for this."

There was a coil of rope lying on top of one of the cupboards. On the rope was another big sign:

Dear Suzie:
Take hold of this rope and swing through the air
with the greatest of ease—to the Lookout.
Love,
Grandfather

Suzie uncoiled the rope, gave a hard kick, and swung through the branches and landed on the Lookout. She called, "Co Co, it's just like Tarzan's Last Leap! I'll swing back so you can try it." She stood on her cupboard, gave a hard kick, and landed beside Co Co.

Co Co swung over to the Lookout, giving loud Tarzan yells. She called out, "Suzie! Quick, quick! There is something here. I will throw the rope. Catch it."

Suzie swung over beside Co Co. In a small basket was another sign:

Dear Suzie:
Try this and see if it works better than yelling.
You can also send Co Co some food.
Love,
Grandfather

They found that Grandfather had made them a basket with a pulley, just like the ones which bring back change in old-fashioned stores. They pulled the basket back and forth several times, and then Suzie said, "Let's go home and give Grandfather the biggest hug he's ever had. Oh, isn't this just the neatest birthday you've ever had in your whole life!"

Co Co's eyes were black with excitement. "It is! Indeed it is! I did not know the birthday could be so wonderful!"

They climbed down the ladder and ran through the orchard, leaping and pushing each other with the sheer delight of a birthday morning. They rushed in and hugged Grandfather until they almost squeezed the breath out of him. They were shouting and laughing and both talking at once, when Grandmother put her finger to her lips. "Shhhh! You might frighten my birthday presents."

She pointed to two baskets, side by side, on the window sill. Peering out from under doll blankets, were two of Smokey's brand-new kittens. "The blue basket is Co Co's and the pink one is yours."

The kitten in the blue basket was jet black with white dots over each eye, white paws, and a white-tipped tail. "Oh, Grand'mère, I shall call mine 'Minette.' He is so little and so charming."

Suzie's kitten was dark gray with white paws and a white nose. "Grandmother, these kittens have the longest fur of all. Aren't they darling? I think I'll call mine 'Mittens,' to match Co Co's."

Smokey was winding in and out and mewing worriedly. Grandmother picked up both kittens. "Smokey is trying to tell you that her kittens are really too young to leave her yet, so if you don't mind, I'll take them down in the basement and put them in her box with the rest of the kittens."

Suzie's mother came in, kissed and hugged them both, and wished them a happy birthday and said they looked entirely different and much older than they had the night before. Her eyes were dancing as she handed them identical packages. "These are to keep track of every word Rich and Ray said and every word you said back."

They opened twin diaries, Suzie's was dark green and Co Co's dark blue. Suzie said, "Oh, Mother, how did you know I've always wanted a diary!"

Co Co hugged Suzie's mother. "For my secret thoughts. Oh, thank you—thank you so much!"

Suzie's mother said, "Co Co, your father called and said he'd be here in a minute, but to warn you that his best present is a surprise, and he can't give it to you until tonight."

They promptly clamored for a hint of the surprise, but she only shook her head and laughed. "I think you are going to like it best of all, but I promised not to give you any hints."

Grandmother told them to sit down and eat some breakfast because they would need food to sustain them through such a wildly exciting day. Co Co immediately began to eat as if she hadn't seen food for twenty-four hours, but Suzie was much too excited to swallow.

Mr. Langdon opened the kitchen door. He sang, "Happy birthday, two times, happy birthday, two times, happy birthday dear daughters, happy birthday to you" and kissed them both and then he kissed *Suzie's mother!*

Suzie was so surprised she couldn't speak. She looked all around to see what everybody else thought, but they were all calmly eating.

"By the way," Mr. Langdon said, "Mrs. Medlin asked me to warn you not to go into her yard or peek over the hedge."

"We're not going to. We're going to spend the whole day writing in our diaries and sending messages and swinging back and forth. Come on, Co Co—we never have to do one scrap of housework on our birthdays."

At twelve o'clock, Grandfather came down with a large lunch basket. He said there was so much fuss going on in the kitchen that he planned to spend the afternoon with them.

Co Co unpacked the basket. "Grand'père, I wish to invite you to be my first guest in my new nest." She sent a message over to Suzie to say that luncheon was now served.

Suzie swung across and dropped down beside them. "Grandfather, do you think you could put a loop in that rope, so we could put one foot in it and have our hands free to carry things back and forth?"

Grandfather said that after lunch he would make the loop and check both platforms to see that everything was in order.

That afternoon, while Grandfather tightened the pulley and tested the rungs of the ladders and made a stirrup in the swinging rope, Co Co and Suzie wrote in their diaries, putting down everything that had happened to them since the day Suzie first found Co Co in the Lookout.

It was almost four o'clock when Grandfather called to them, "Mother thinks you'd better start getting ready, because some of your guests just might come early."

They climbed hastily down the ladder and Grandfather took their hands and rushed them through the orchard so fast their feet barely touched the ground.

The kitchen was full of platters and delicious smells. Before they even got a good look, Suzie's mother warned, "You'll have to hurry. Mrs. Medlin asked Miss Morrison to bring the children here first, so she could tell them about the party. Now scoot!"

Co Co was finishing her bath, and Suzie was jerking clothes over her wet back when they heard voices. "Oh my gosh, they're here! Hurry up, Co Co!"

Co Co promptly rubbed soap in her eyes, reached wildly for a washcloth, and said, "Help me, quick, quick!"

"Oh, what'll Miss Morrison think?" Suzie helped Co Co out of the tub and began scrubbing at her with a towel. "Don't wait to get dry, just put your clothes on. What if we're not even dressed when Mrs. Medlin is ready for us. Oh, dear!"

In spite of their wailing, they finished dressing in record time and stood side by side in front of the mirror. Suzie breathed, "Aren't these dresses beautiful?" and Co Co raised her eyebrows, and said, "Very, very chic! We do look like the movie stars."

Then they took hold of hands and walked slowly down the front stairs, pointing their toes like models. The whole class was standing in the front hall singing, "Happy birthday to Suzie, happy birthday to Co Co. Happy birthday to Suzie-and-Co Co, Happy birthday to both-of-you." But Suzie and Co Co were too surprised to thank them, for Creamy and Blonde, the puppies from the pound, were curled up side by side on the bottom step!

Rich said, "The puppies are from us," and Ray said "Your mother and father said you could have them and we bought them with our own money. The baskets and stuff are from the whole class. We'll come over and help you train them."

Co Co said, "Thank you. Thank you very much. Rich, you are kind. I know how much you wanted a puppy."

Rich grinned. "Think nothing of it. We already have two dogs and you haven't any yet. He'll be okay with you if we help train him."

Suzie thanked Ray and said it certainly was nice of him to get the puppy for her, especially when he wanted it so much.

Rich and Ray helped Suzie and Co Co carry the puppies and baskets down to the basement, and on the way back Ray took Suzie's arm. "That sure is a neat dress. Both you and Co Co look—uh—pretty."

Suzie's cheeks got quite pink and the tickly smile dimpled around her mouth again as she thanked him.

They joined the group. The boys, at one end of the living room, were punching each other and grinning. The girls were clustered together at the other end, giggling and admiring one another's party dresses.

Mrs. Medlin came in, leaning on a cane. They all stood up and said in chorus, "How do you do, Mrs. Medlin."

Mrs. Medlin walked around and shook hands with each child. "You are Sumiko"—"You are Marjorie"— "You are Johnny Allen"—"You are Rich and Ray."

Not once did she make a mistake.

Then she asked them all to sit down, took a notebook out of her purse, and in her regular cross-teacher voice, began: "Listen to me carefully, and please don't interrupt. I don't wish to get mixed up. First, there will be swimming in Co Co's pool."

There was a rustle of approval and she held up her hand. "Children, *please* don't interrupt. If you do, I am liable to serve ice cream first and hot soup for dessert."

Suzie and Co Co laughed, but the rest of the class sat perfectly still and stared at her.

"The girls will change their clothes in Suzie's house and the boys at Co Co's house." They started toward the door, but Mrs. Medlin held up her hand again. "Just a moment, *please!*" They all stopped just as if they were playing statue. "You must *not* go through the orchard or into my yard. There are things there which I *don't* want you to see. After you have had your swim, you may come to me, and I'll tell you what to do next. All right, you may go."

They began filing out of the room, just as if they were in school. "Boy! She sounds as if we were stepping on her flower beds. Didn't she want to give your party or what?" Dorothy whispered.

Suzie answered, "She sounds crabby, but she's really neat. You wait. You'll see. Co Co and I just love her."

They ran upstairs and hurried into their bathing suits. When they arrived at Co Co's pool, the boys were already diving, splashing, and yelling. Mrs. Medlin called from the terrace, "Suzie, you and Co Co come and get these beach balls. They are the prizes for the boy and girl who are the best at water polo. *Don't* start 'til I get there."

By the time she had umpired the game, which Sumiko and Johnny Allen won, had asked each of them to line up and dive for her, and praised each one extravagantly in the same abrupt cross voice, the children knew that Mrs. Medlin was a good friend who understood them.

They clustered around her, laughing and joking, just as if they'd always known her, and Suzie said, proudly, "See what I mean? She's just about the neatest grown-up we've ever met."

Then Mrs. Medlin told them all to pay attention and took out her notebook. "You'll probably get tired of changing your clothes, but I couldn't figure out any other way to do this. Did you all bring your jeans?" They nodded and smiled. "Now see how fast you can put them on. Don't dawdle. I'll meet you all on my front porch."

After they'd put on their jeans, they walked down the sidewalk to Mrs. Medlin's front gate. Bravo, looking very proud and haughty, met them. He was wearing a large pink bow on his topknot and was brushed within an inch of his life. There was a howl of derisive laughter from the class when they saw him, but without even wagging his tail, Bravo turned and led them to the front door.

Mrs. Medlin said, "As you all know, I have been very inconsiderate of children and dogs. To show you that I am sorry, I have tried to make this party as much fun as I possibly could. This game is a combination of Spider Web, a game I used to enjoy when I was your age, and Treasure Hunt, a game I'm sure you've all played. There are clues and prizes and a main treasure. You may help one another if you wish."

The children started to talk and giggle, but Mrs. Medlin held up her hand. "*Please!* Now line up and take the clothespin and flashlight with your name on it. You wind the string on the clothespin until you reach your clue. That's the end of the string. Read the clue and figure out where the treasure is hidden. Remember, there is a main treasure, too, which you will have to find. When all the prizes are found, you may change your clothes. Supper will be ready when you are. Are there any questions? Very well. Ready— get set—go!"

They found their clothespins and flashlights and began to wind. They wound and wound and wound, over and under branches, in and out of trees and back and forth between the gardens. They bumped heads and crawled on their hands and knees and climbed trees.

They had been winding for about half an hour, when Barbara called out, "I've found my clue! Come here, everybody!"

Tied to her string was a little card which read: "I rest my head on a leafy bed."

Suzie said, "The only leafy bed I can think of is the compost pit." They followed Barbara to the pit and, sure enough, there was her present with her name on it.

It was a long-playing record. "Oh baby! For my collection!" She ran back and thanked Mrs. Medlin and offered to help anybody else who was stuck.

Johnny's clue was next: "A dog's best friend, is your string's end." On the back porch, right by Bravo's feeding dish was Johnny's present. A dog collar and leash, which he had been saving for since Christmas.

Then the clues began to come thick and fast, and there were screams of "Come here, everybody!" from all over the garden. The children agreed that Mrs. Medlin must be a mind reader because each present proved to be something they had been talking about and saving for.

It was getting dark and the flickering light of the flashlights winked and blinked like lightning bugs as they all followed Suzie and Co Co, who were still patiently winding, toward the old apple tree by the back porch. Rich offered to climb the tree and he brought down two clues. Suzie read hers first:

"I like the warm dark summer night
When fireflies burn their golden light
And flit so softly through the air
Now up, now down, now over there!
They sparkle in my apple tree—"

And Co Co continued:

"And from the grass, they wink at me
And turn their lights on one by one
I think it would be lots of fun
If I could shine at evening too,

Just as the little fireflies do."

Ray said, "It's hidden in the grass. Hurry up everybody before it gets so dark we can't see."

They were all crawling on their hands and knees in the orchard, when the whole garden was lighted by strings of swinging Japanese lanterns. They danced in swaying colorful rows through the trees and over into Mrs. Medlin's garden and into the trees in Co Co's yard. There was a long-drawn-out "Ohhhh!" from the class when Suzie and Co Co saw their presents lying right where they had been camping the night they rescued Mrs. Medlin. They were two charm bracelets with little pagodas, goldfish, dragons, and Chinese junks, just like the pictures on the dancing lanterns.

In the bottom of Suzie's box was a note which said:

Everybody's ball of string,
Winds up at the garden swing.

And in the bottom of Co Co's box was a note saying:

Now put on your party clothes,
You're probably hungry, goodness knows.
The Wicked Witch

They rushed down to the Lookout and hanging on

the swing was a huge bunch of long sparklers with a note which read:

These are for after supper.
Hurry up—I'm hungry.
Mrs. M.

They changed their clothes again and walked down to Co Co's terrace, as formally as if they were attending a ball. There was another long-drawn-out "Ohhhh!" as they saw the Pink House. The pool shone with reflections from the swaying, twinkling Japanese lanterns, the record player had been moved out into the patio and was playing dance music, and the long table was decorated with flags and huge bunches of Roman candles, rockets, flares, and all sorts of fireworks.

Suzie looked down the long table. Mr. Wagner had come and Grandmother and Grandfather and everybody looked happy and excited. The dresses were so pretty and the boys looked so neat and well-groomed. It wasn't exactly like a movie party, but it was a whole lot more fun.

Just then Mrs. MacGregor came out carrying a turkey, snapping and sizzling with twenty-four long sparklers. As she placed it in front of Mr. Langdon she said, "This is my present—a Fourth of July birthday turkey." She also had ice cream with red, white, and blue stripes, and a huge birthday cake with flags instead of candles.

After dinner, Mr. Langdon shot off the fireworks over the pool. Roman candles whooshed up in the air and exploded in showers of stars. Catherine wheels sent brilliant colored sparks up into the trees until they twinkled like Christmas trees. The music sang through Suzie's arms and rippled on her skin; the lanterns danced in her eyes. She leaned against her mother and said, "Oh, Mother, I'm so glad about the Pink House and Co Co and Mr. Langdon. I'm so happy I can't even tell you."

Suzie's Mother said, "I'm happy, too, darling. Happier than I've ever been before, I think."

After the fireworks were over, it was almost ten o'clock and Mrs. Medlin called out, "*Don't* go home yet. I want you to light these sparklers you found in the swing and stand around the pool, waving them over the water. I'm going to stand on the bridge and take some pictures of the very best party I've ever been to."

They did just as they were told, and as they stood around the pool, they called, "Hooray for Mrs. Medlin. Thanks for the wonderful party! Hooray for Mrs. Medlin!" until her eyes were so misty with tears she couldn't see to take the pictures.

Then they all collected their clothes and their

presents and started home with cheers for Mrs. Medlin ringing through the summer night.

After everyone had left, Mr. Langdon said it was almost time for his surprise and if Co Co and Suzie would go and get into bed at the Pink House, just at midnight, he and Suzie's mother would come in and tell them the surprise.

They ran back to Grandmother's and got Suzie's suitcase, and then decided to sleep in the twin beds in Co Co's room so they could talk about the party until midnight.

It was almost midnight when Co Co said, "Suzie, let us go to the Lookout and watch the lanterns and listen to the music. We are like Cinderella and we must see the party once more."

So they crawled out the window and sneaked around the back of the house and climbed up into the Lookout. By crawling out on a branch and leaning way over, they could see the patio and watch the grown people.

Co Co chuckled. "Listen, Monsieur Wagner is speaking of love to Mademoiselle Morrison. He tells her she is beautiful and . . ."

"Shhhh! Mother is telling your father something."

Suzie's mother was standing almost below them. She smiled up at Co Co's father. "I have always been sure, Bill. After all, I've been in love with you since I was fifteen years old, but I didn't realize it. Now we must tell the children."

Co Co gasped. "Suzie! We are the dumb, dopey knotheads! The arranged marriage!"

"Gosh all fish hooks!" With one lithe movement, they dropped down in front of their astonished parents.

"Is this the present? Will you really be my chère maman?

"Do we all get to live in the Pink House?"

"Will Suzie be my sister?"

"Oh, isn't this neat?"

"It is indeed, neat and keen!"

Suzie's mother kissed them both. "We are going to be married next week, darlings, and I am so happy I can hardly speak!"

But Mr. Langdon caught them all up in a big bear hug. "At last, we'll all be Langdons and we'll all be best friends."

About the Author

Like Co Co in *Best Friends*, **Mary Bard** moved frequently as a child due to her father's job. She attended kindergarten in Mexico City, first grade in New York, and second grade in Colorado. Later, she went to college at the University of Washington in Seattle, and she eventually settled with her family in the Seattle area. *Best Friends* is the first of three novels about Suzie and Co Co, which were published through the 1950s and 60s. Bard also wrote three autobiographical works for adults: *Just Be Yourself*, *The Doctor Wears Three Faces*, and *Forty Odd*.

NANCY PEARL PRESENTS A BOOK CRUSH REDISCOVERY